The Man
With No Skin

by
Órfhlaith Ní Chonaill

PUBLISHING, INC.

First cloth printing: 2005
ISBN: 0-9764904-9-8
LCCN: 2005922039

Dialogue Publishing
16990 Cherry Crossing Dr.
Colorado Springs, CO 80921
http://www.dialoguepublishing.com
info@dialoguepublishing.com

Editing and book layout by Dorrie O'Brien, Arlington, Texas
Cover design by Gail Cross, Desert Isle Design, Mesa, Arizona

Printed in the United States of America

1 2 3 4 5 6 7 8 9 10

For Robin, my love, with thanks.

1

A Mercedes with dark windows drove up one day and parked between the speed bumps on the road beside Kishagi Market. A fat man got out of the passenger side and leaned for a while on the roof of the car, surveying the scene and consulting a large white sheet of paper. He was one of "themselves," obviously—a member of the tribe, although nobody could put a name on him or say exactly which clan he belonged to. The dark sunglasses he wore did not help identification. He puffed on a cigar and spoke to no one, or no one spoke to him, which was unusual, but he had an air of importance about him. He had the girth of a man who was prosperous. His immaculate, European-style suit and tie, added to the Merc, which was obviously chauffeur-driven, spoke of wealth and power that would intimidate the bravest of this small community. Neither the vegetable woman nor the sandal-maker recognized him or found the courage to ask him his business.

For a full three minutes, the stranger leaned on the

roof of his car, looking out over the acre or so of make-shift wooden-and-thatch stalls that made up the Kishagi marketplace. He must have seen the woman at her open-fronted stall with the vegetables displayed across the entrance: potatoes in triangular piles, bundles of carrots, stacks of green avocados, bright heaps of pineapples, sweet potatoes, watermelons, pumpkins, and yellow bananas still on their stalks and hanging from the roof.

Maybe he noticed the sandal-maker cutting up old tires with a sharp knife and crafting the rubber pieces into soles and straps, his eyes watching everything and everyone warily.

If he had walked along the narrow aisles between the overhanging, banana-leaf-thatched roofs, he would have found a market that was neatly enough laid out as markets went. He would have seen the small drains that ran alongside the stalls. Maybe he would have met old Wairimu sitting on a stool beside an open sack of rice—pouring fistfuls into her apron and picking through the grains for stones and impurities.

Farther along, he would have heard the whir of a sewing machine in the space behind a window and found the tailor sewing suits and trousers, blouses and dresses, the plain and patterned cloths cut and ready for orders taken in advance.

At another stall that had woolen cardigans hanging outside, he would have found the knitters inside with their knitting needles. If he had asked, they would have made him up a cardigan for his wife, or a woolen waist coat for himself, maybe, and charged him very little in comparison to the prices in the city shops. Even farther along, he would have heard a choir practicing. He could have found the choirmaster clunking out the notes on a little toy piano to give the sopranos, altos, and basses the proper notes for their harmonies.

Next, he would have come to the Kishagi Hoteli where the proprietor had used flattened Coca-Cola cans to improvise a shiny red shop front. Inside, he could have drunk his fill of warm, bottled beer under the twin logos, *Baada ya Kazi* "after work," and *Bia na Bora*, "the best beer." He could even have had a bottled Guinness, mixed in a tumbler with Coca-Cola. The patrons might have regaled him with stories of the latest news of here and of the larger world. Someone might have bought him a drink, or scrounged one. The tantalizing smell of roasting chicken and goat might have tempted him to eat meat with his beer, and the proprietor would have brought a jug of water for him to wash his hands.

At the end of that row, he would have reached the stall that sold African cloths, each with its own slogan written in Swahili. If there were a breeze, he would have seen the beautiful, multicolored rectangles of cloth billowing like huge flags. He could have visited the potter's stall and bought freshly-made terra-cotta pots in any shape or size for domestic or decorative use. In another

stall, he might have met a group of stall-holders having
their lunch of *irio*–potato mashed with maize, beans,
and greens. Or *sukuma wiki*–spinach fried with onion
and tomato. He might have met the cool dude who had
returned from America with the Rastafarian extensions
and the big Jamaican hat. He sold transistor radios in
his stall, blaring out reggae music in competition with
the local radio station blasting from the bar, with the
local musician, Queen Jane, piping, high-pitched and
rhythmic, from the tailor's shop and with the choir's
fitful harmonies.

Even from where he stood, he must have heard a
cacophony of these sounds, along with the crowing of a
cock and the cackle of hens from the stall that had
"Life Chicken" written over it. And he would have heard
the babble of voices raised in argument and bargaining.
From here, too, he could have smelled the unique odor
of the place: the mix of rotting fruit, drains, and roasting food. He would have glimpsed something of the life
that had been happening in this place for as long as
anyone could remember.

But the stranger folded up his sheet of paper and
the chauffeur drove away. His visit evoked some curiosity but little real suspicion. He had taken a wrong turn
off the highway, they said, and was consulting his map
to see where he had gone astray.

Of course afterward, people would say that they had
recognized him instantly, that he was the henchman of a

well-known politician. Others would say that he was the politician himself. But that was after the notice appeared.

The sign had been erected overnight and stood just at the entrance to the market. PRIVATE PROPERTY, it read. SQUATTERS WILL BE EVICTED. BY ORDER— The signature was an illegible squiggle.

I was sitting outside on the veranda finishing my morning cup of tea when I looked up and was amused at first to see Nicolas the sacristan running up the road. I had never before seen Nicolas run. Then I noticed how agitated he was. He was so breathless he could barely talk.

"Baba, Baba, it's the marketplace—it has been grabbed."

"Grabbed? How? By whom?"

"They say it is some big bwana."

Land-grabbing was something I read about constantly in the newspapers. It involved the illegitimate selling of land already legitimately owned. It was an elaborate hoax usually perpetrated by unscrupulous businessmen or politicians. People parted with their money only to find that the land that they had bought was already legally owned. Often, both buyer and owner came up against an impossible brick wall of bureaucracy when they tried to solve the dispute. Land-grabbing usually happened in remote places where the ownership of the land was dubious anyway. I hadn't expected it to happen here, in

Kishagi, where every inch of ground was jealously guarded and had been owned and passed from generation to generation for hundreds of years.

A meeting was called in the Highway Motel. As I was buttoning on my collar to go, John Kariuki, the deacon, came into the room.

"Father O'Sullivan," he said, "do you think you should be seen to be involved in something political like this?"

"Political?" I caught my grin in the mirror and the anxious face of Kariuki behind me. Then I grimaced, struggling with the button and the stiff, rarely-worn collar. "Most likely 'twas some smart fellow locally who drew up documents for the site, and sold them to somebody for a bundle of money. It's probably not even legal, not to mind political."

"They say it is some politician who drove up in his car and made the order."

"Which politician?"

"There are different accounts."

"Well, Kariuki, if they had seen him, you would think they would know who he was, wouldn't you?"

I watched him wince at my use of the familiar name, Kariuki. Since he had come back from the seminary, he had been calling himself John. Father John, the locals called him, not understanding the distinction between priest and deacon. Kariuki had been actively encouraging the misnomer.

"We priests—" He stopped himself, catching the lift of my eyebrows in the mirror. "We . . . need to look to the spiritual needs of our flock, not to their physical or political concerns."

"For God's sake, Kariuki! Do you expect me not to back the people on this one?" With a gesture of frustration, I tossed the non-compliant collar on the bed and headed out.

A large crowd had gathered in the courtyard of the motel—the only three-story building in Kishagi. It was higher than the church, I reckoned, by at least a meter. The courtyard was surrounded by a high wall and, as I entered through the gate, the smell of roasting meat wafted out from the kitchens. The village elders, tradespeople, stall-holders from the market, and plenty of curious onlookers were huddled around small tables and everyone was talking excitedly.

"A drink, Father?" an old man called to me in greeting.

"Thanks, Mzee." The Mzee brought the beer and I sat with him at the elders' table. A dish was placed in front of us. Water was poured out of a jug for us to wash our hands. We dipped our fingers into the dish and chewed on the tastiest delicacy of the roasting goat: the white meat of the intestines.

As we chewed, we debated the problem. There were as many versions of the story as there were people, it seemed, but the elders agreed that the decree could certainly not be legal. The ownership of the plot was clear

under the customary law: There was no question that
the land had ever been vacant or had ever been designated "Government Land"; therefore, it was unlikely that
the decree had come from a high political level, or that
an eviction order could be legitimate vis-à-vis the law of
the land.

When the debate was opened to everyone, there were
some impassioned speeches from the other tables. The
proprietor of the Kishagi Hoteli said that the great
Mogai, the divider of the universe, had designated that
land as the Kishagi marketplace and, since remembered
time had begun, his ancestors had traded there. Old
Wairimu said that the land was the mother of the tribe.
It gave sustenance and life to the people during all their
lives and took to itself the bodies of the ancestors. Therefore, it was sacred and nobody had the right to violate
or steal Gikuyu land. The sandal-maker said that he and
his brothers were the proper owners of the site according to the common law, but that his ancestors had willed
that it should be used by the people of Kishagi as a
marketplace. It was his pleasure and the pleasure of his
brothers to allow the use of their land for their tribesmen. They had never asked for rent because they were
privileged to give it for free for the good of their people.
But if these grabbers came and took their land from
them, then the ancestors would be displeased and the
consequences would be terrible.

My wandering eye caught John Kariuki in the crowd,

his face set in a frown of disapproval at the tone of what was being said. He was embarrassed at what he would have considered "primitive" talk, particularly in my presence. But I had been privy to many meetings and transactions in Kishagi and I had learned to know and respect the traditional wisdom of the tribe.

The vegetable woman said that Kishagi Market was the center of the whole district, much more so than this nice motel and more so even than the church. She looked sheepishly at me as she said that.

"Yes," I agreed with her. "The marketplace has been here much longer than the church has." I looked up and saw again John Kariuki's frown. No doubt all of this would be reported back verbatim to the bishop.

Mzee Njuguna got up and addressed the assembly. His gray hairs and whiskers were a badge of his age and wisdom and had earned him the title Mzee—wise man. There was absolute silence as he spoke.

"We do not know who has placed an eviction order on Kishagi Market. We cannot know from where this order came, whether it is the work of someone in power, or if it is a money-making trick by some person from our village or elsewhere. Kishagi Market has indeed been the property of Kamau's family of the Kishagi Hoteli for generations, since the first dividing of the land. Whether the land was ever registered officially under the new law, we do not know. Only that under the common law it belongs to him and to his brothers for the communal use of all of us. We will seek the services of a barrister to explain our legal position. But we cannot fight for our right to ownership until this person who has made this order makes himself known to us. The eviction notice will be removed from the spot. If someone wants to serve the notice legally, they will have to confront us, the elders, as trustees for the people.

"We have decided to lobby all the politicians, especially those who have been suspected of involvement in this eviction order. If they are not the guilty ones, then let them come and give us their support."

A cheer of approval burst through the crowd. The Mzee raised his hand for quiet and continued. "All of us at this table will sign these letters to the politicians. Baba Kilani has agreed to sign along with us, to give the letters more weight." "Baba Kilani" was a title based on a mispronunciation of my Christian name, Ciarán, and was what I was cordially called throughout the district. Kariuki was the only one who ever used my surname, O'Sullivan. At the sudden memory of him in the crowd, I called out: "John Kariuki."

"What's that, Baba?" the Mzee asked.

"Father John might wish to sign the letters."

There was a twinkle in the old man's eye as he turned away from me; Kariuki's views were well known around the parish.

"Fatha John, Fatha John, Fatha John," the chant went round. Kariuki was found and forced to stand up, red-faced.

"Will you sign the letters, Father John?"

Kariuki glared at me as he assented.

"All right," the Mzee said, "that has been agreed. Now, meantime, we will post two watchmen on Kishagi Market at all times, until this trouble is over."

It was the darkest hour of night and the watchmen were in their hut at the center of Kishagi Market. Suddenly, the door banged closed and the bolt slammed shut from the outside, locking them in. Nobody in the village heard their cries for help. Soon their voices were smothered in a crackling rush of flames and timbers burning. Smoke seeped in through the gaps in the shed walls and the two men were overcome by the smoke.

The attackers must have moved swiftly down through the aisles, pouring paraffin in wide arcs, throwing a lighted match here, another one there. The sandal-maker's stall caught fire, the rubber took shortly afterward, causing huge flames to leap into the air. The smell of burning rubber choked the night air, waking the village dogs, which set up a fierce barking, alerting the cockerels in the dead of night. Cock-a-doodle-*doo*. Cock-a-doodle-*doo*!

People were disturbed from their sleep and rushed out of their homes to see what was wrong. Nicolas ran into the church and set the bell ringing. It was the peal of the bell that woke me. I smelled the smoke and heard the cries of "Fire! Fire!" Barely pausing to drag on a pair of trousers, shirt, and sandals, I hurried down. An eerie glow had taken possession of the sky above Kishagi.

I joined the gathering crowd. We moved in toward

the front, toward the sandal-maker's stall, but were driven back by the flames, the smoke, and the intense heat of the burning rubber.

"The watchmen, the watchmen," someone shouted and we moved en masse to the far side of the market, which was not yet burning fiercely. I saw two men pull jumpers over their heads and disappear into the billowing smoke. They reappeared, dragging the still figure of one of the watchmen. Then they dashed back in and rescued the other, just in time, as that whole area of the market succumbed to the flames. After some resuscitation, both watchmen coughed and spluttered and gasped their way back to consciousness. Apart from smoke inhalation, they were unharmed. A shout of relief echoed on the smoky air.

I saw old Wairimu watching and crying aloud as her little stall turned orange, then yellow, then collapsed into gray and guttered out to nothing. The smoke was acrid now. People made vain attempts to throw water on the flames but could not get close enough to the source, as the eddies of flame and heat rushed toward them. The fire was like a wild thing leaping in a macabre fit of destruction. It consumed everything in its path. The deep yellow of the central flame was spreading across the small alleys, shedding orange flickers of flame from roof to roof. I could have almost described them as beautiful if it weren't for the shocking loss of so many people's livelihoods.

Most of the market was ablaze now. Nothing more could be saved from any of the stalls. Kerosene and gas canisters exploded here and there, sending showers of sparks into the night sky. Timbers fell with a crash and a shoot of flame. With each explosion and collapse, the crowd gasped and wailed, surged forward to survey the devastation for themselves but drew back again from the intense heat. Was it my imagination or could I distinguish the smell of burning wool above all else burning? I thought of the cardigan shop. I pictured the Kishagi Hoteli with the beer bottles bursting, the roof caving in, the flattened Coke cans falling and warping in the heat. I thought of sparks dropping down and setting the sheet music ablaze in the stall where the choir usually practiced. Found myself wondering if the little toy piano had been left there to burn.

Suddenly Mzee Njuguna was at my side, tugging my sleeve. "Baba, come quickly. They have caught the attackers. God help them."

We ran in the direction from which he had come. As we ran, I could hear the angry roaring of men. My feet were heavy as if bogged down in the earth. I prayed that we would be in time. The chant: "Burn them, burn them, burn them," resounded in my ears.

We came to the back of the crowd and I shouted: "Stop, stop," as I tried to push my way through. But the shoulders ranked together to block my way. Jumping up to see above the crowd, I caught a glimpse of two men.

Tires had been slung around their necks. "No. No. Stop! Don't do this," I yelled.

But my voice was as nothing against the jeering and taunting of the crowd and the ever-present chant: "Burn them, burn them, burn them."

The resistance to my pressure eased. I found my way through as the mob dissipated. In the instant that the match was lit, they dispersed. I barely saw who they were. Suddenly there was just myself and Mzee Njuguna. And two men on fire. I recognized them both: locals from the village.

The smell of burning wool, rubber, kerosene, and timber was nothing to the stench of human flesh burning. Incredibly, they were still standing, running, screaming, their hair singed off, their heads ablaze. Their arms flailed as if they were involved in some strange dance. One of the men's ears melted. He fell and lay on the ground, writhing and screaming. I knelt by him and tried to beat the flames out with my hands, but his skin stuck to me.

"Save your hands for praying, Baba Kilani," the Mzee said gently. "Do not try to stop them burning. You will only make their suffering longer and harder."

I prayed over the dying men, but I felt my prayers were unnecessary. Even the death of Christ on the cross seemed lesser agony than what I saw those men endure. When it was over, their wives were called. One man was identified by a ring he wore on his finger, the other by a brass buckle on his belt.

***

A policeman called at the church compound the next morning. He walked quietly, self-consciously, keeping a watchful eye around him and holding his rifle in both hands as if he half expected to be attacked. "It has been reported that bandits looted and burned the market. Two watchmen on duty were killed. Is that correct?"

"Watchmen?"

"Yes," he said brusquely. "The two who were burnt in the shed. Can I see them?"

I took him to the church and lifted the lids off the two makeshift coffins, the coffin-maker having refused to be involved. The policeman inspected the remains.

"Are these two men known to you?"

"Yes."

"Have their bodies been identified by their relatives?"

"They have."

"What are their names?" He wrote them down. "And these were the two watchmen? The ones who were locked in the shed?"

"Yes."

If, on the Day of Judgement, I were charged with this lie, I would defend it to my Maker, I decided, rather than implicate so many men in my parish. What good would it do to have them locked up to die of dysentery in an overcrowded jail? What did I know of last night's events, anyway? In the heat and the confusion, what could I really swear to have seen? Was that Irungu's face

I saw through a haze of black smoke? Was that the sandal-maker? Was that the Rastafarian? Could I be sure?
Would any of it stand scrutiny or cross-examination?

"Will you take me to the shed where they were locked
in?"

We walked together down to the speed bumps and
stood on the road looking at the smoking, blackened,
and charred field.

"It was somewhere toward the middle. One of a row
of five or six. There's nothing left of it."

The policeman shook his head. "Way," he said, sadly.
And then in a tone of deep frustration: "Way-aay-aay.
Everywhere, it is the same. These bandits come in the
night and nobody can know who they are or where they
come from. Or where they will strike next. They are
very bad men." He clicked the heels of his boots together and turned to walk down to the highway from
where he would hitch a ride back to his station.

John Kariuki was waiting anxiously for me in the church
compound. "What did you tell the police?"

I greeted him coldly. "That's none of your business,
Kariuki. You'd better go and get ready for the funerals."

He stood self-consciously, jigging from one foot to
the other. "I . . . I cannot go."

"You're the one who's always going on about duty.
Well, this time it's your duty to give these poor fellows
a Christian burial and to stand up publicly and condemn their murders."

"No." There was a vein throbbing on Kariuki's temple. He looked at me shiftily, then looked down at the ground. "I cannot go. I have been threatened—"

"Kariuki, d'you know something? I believe you'd deny a man a drink of water to save his life so that you could save his soul and hasten his way to Heaven."

"The souls of our parishioners are our concern. Not their lives."

"And what do you think of our fine fellows here?" I gestured at the locked door of the church where the alleged arsonists were reposing in death. "Do you think they're in Heaven?"

He shook his head slowly. "I do not think they deserve it."

"Even after the horrific deaths that were imposed on them? Do you know what I think, Kariuki? I think that any poor fellow who went through what those men did deserves Heaven. It was murder. You can't condone it."

"I do not condone it."

"You'll condemn it then?"

"I cannot condemn it."

"Kariuki, you're a miserable little coward."

A small group, mostly women, gathered in Kishagi church that day for the funerals. The village elders arrived in a show of solidarity. Perhaps nobody would threaten them. But I suspected that Mzee Njuguna, as a fair-minded man who disapproved of murder, would have turned up anyway.

The sound of fierce weeping from the front rows told the story of the widows and their children, clutching each other, trying to make sense of what had happened or what their loved ones had done that had brought such devastation and shame on their lives.

I looked out over the sad and sober faces of this small congregation and I addressed them: "These men who are lying here are innocent victims. Doing a desperate thing, surely—a cruel and horrible thing, but small people doing it for the money. Are their children hungry? Did anyone ask what problems drove these men to do what they did? Are they such sinners as we think them to be? Perhaps they were not the ones who burned the market. How can we know? They protested their innocence. Maybe they were there to steal because there was no food at home. Or maybe they were just trying to save something from the market for somebody else. They have not been given the benefit of a jury or a judge or a court of law. Some men of this village decided to take the law into their own hands. But is it our place to judge them? Now that they have been murdered, can't we leave judgement to God?

"And even if these men were the ones who burned the market, we need to ask, who did they work for? Do we know? Who is the big bwana who is claiming this land? Is his claim legitimate? Does he think his claim is legitimate? We should ask is he the bad one, or is there another faceless one behind him? An unscrupulous man, who sold land that wasn't his to sell? Or a politician falsifying deeds? You have looked in the wrong place for the guilty. You have murdered the innocent. It is not right to kill. You will, all of you, be judged on what you have done today. Not just the ones who brought the tire. Not just the one who poured the petrol. Not just the one who lit the match. But all of you. Each one of you who believed these men should die. Each one who shouted out that they were guilty. Each one who chanted 'burn them!' Every one of us who was there, who stood back and allowed it to happen. Even I feel tainted by your guilt.

"And now that they are dead, now that they are beyond the savage deaths you imposed upon them, you must allow God to judge them. It is not up to you to judge if they are worthy to inhabit Christian ground. It is only God who has the right to judge them and I suspect that these men will find forgiveness from a just and loving God. If Hell was what was in store for them, you have already purged them with the agony of the deaths you imposed upon them.

"I know that many of the guilty are absent from the church, but I entrust my words to you to be delivered to them."

2

The great mountain was hiding itself. At a glance, it seemed there was no mountain there at all—only a gray tent of clouds rising into the blue sky.

Wambui stood, her feet apart, as if planted in the red earth. Her body was bent over in an inverted V-shape, legs absolutely straight, bottom uppermost, her trunk slanted down to where her hands were planting seedlings in the fertile ground of the *shamba*. She was a slender girl, her skin black and glowing. Her full bosom was heavy and brimming with milk for her boy-child, who lay asleep against her back. She and the baby were bound together with a swathe of African cloth which was knotted at her stomach and shoulder. The vivid yellow and purple cloth enveloped the child completely, covering even his head from the fierce rays of the afternoon sun. Wambui straightened up. Her hand went instinctively to hold the baby as she moved.

She bent again and continued with her work, her right hand slitting open the soil with the blade of the *jembe*, her left deftly slipping each plant into place and closing the earth tenderly around it. She never looked back at what she had planted, but moved along, slowly and meticulously, in a perfectly straight line, over to the perimeter hedge, then back along the next furrow.

As she turned again, her eyes were drawn to the tallest of the banana trees. It was in the shade of that tree that Irungu had sat, making his plans for the *shamba*.

"We will plant the maize there," he had said, indicating the area she was now working, "and the orchard will be over there."

She glanced across at the cluster of young banana, avocado, and orange trees, all thriving under her care.

"And at the back we'll have rabbits and hens."

The wooden frames of the hutches were just visible behind the house.

"And if we have a good crop of maize, we will build a stone house with a tin roof."

"A house like Shiku's!" she'd said, joyously. "With stone walls and glass windows." She would be so proud to live in a house like that.

She could remember Irungu exactly as he was on that day. She could see him, her husband, his sensual lips and his handsome face under that old straw hat of his. His dark eyes had twinkled and glowed as he had spelled out his plans. Then he had lowered his head to concentrate on the piece of wood that he was carving. Even when he was relaxed, Irungu's hands were never still: always whittling away at pieces of wood, creating shapes of animals and birds.

"What is it you are making, Irungu?" she had asked.

"Ngai, god of the mountain," he had answered, smiling up at her.

The blade of his knife was working round and round a single point, sharpening it like the tip of a spear.

"I know," she had said. "Ngai, the warrior, coming to destroy the people who have forsaken him for the Christian god!" It was a constant theme of Irungu's.

He had smiled. "Wait. You will see."

When he had finished carving, he inspected his creation, then handed it to her.

As Wambui took the effigy, she laughed. The little figure had laughed back at her—its teeth open in an enormous grin.

Holding Ngai in her hand, she had seen the sharp point she had thought might be a spear. It was Ngai's phallus, erect and jutting out beneath his pot belly. At the back, Irungu had carved a tiny pair of buttocks.

"Now, I know why Ngai is so happy!" Wambui's laughter shook the leaves of the banana tree.

"He is like I am when you are beside me." Irungu's grin was as broad as Ngai's and he had pulled her down beside him on the ground.

"You," she had scolded him. "You pretend to respect tradition, but if you really did, you would say that this is taboo." She had smiled provocatively as she spoke and run a finger gently up and down his chest.

"But it is your duty to bear children for the conti-
nuity of the tribe."

"By carrying on like this in the middle of the day?"
she had mocked. "Ngai might laugh, but he would not
approve!"

"Pah," he had spat. "To hell with Ngai!"

Still feigning protest, Wambui had followed him into
the house. It always used to be like that with Irungu. So
much fun. There was a wildness in him that she loved.
It was part of his charm.

But she had been proved right in what she had said
about him. Irungu had no respect for tradition—or anything. She looked with disgust at the dry stalks of last
season's maize, standing taller than herself. She had
picked and burnt most of them, returning the ashes as
fertilizer to the soil. But that was Irungu's job. He had
promised to do his share. She had left some straggly
stalks behind for him, as reminders of his neglect.

She let a wave of disappointment and anger well
inside her as she looked up at the circular straw hut that
was still her home. It had been a good maize crop. Irungu
must have fetched plenty of money for it in the market
in Nairobi. Not one shilling had come back to her.

Wambui straightened again and squinted up to where
the mountain was hidden. She wondered if those clouds
would bring rain to settle in her newly planted seedlings.
Maybe Ngai was visiting his mountain now and would
see her need. Maybe he would not. He was a fickle god,

that one. Anyway, she didn't believe in all that superstition. If her plants needed water, she would draw it herself from the new water scheme in the village.

Wambui paused in her work as a movement caught her eye. A blue and green bus had pulled in below at the road and a familiar figure was alighting. Her aunt, Wairimu, was back from the city.

Leaving her *jembe* and sheltering the unplanted seedlings from the sun, Wambui hurried down the lane to meet her aunt. Old Wairimu had begun the steep ascent. On her back was a heavy bag, which was anchored to her forehead by a long strap. Her frail body stooped forward under the strain. She had a live chicken tucked under her arm and an array of brightly-colored plastic bags.

Wambui took the smaller bags from her. "What news of your journey, Tata?"

"Fine, very fine," her aunt replied. "What news of yourself?"

"Quite fine. What news of Nairobi?"

"Fine."

Wambui bit back the question that was uppermost on her tongue. All the usual pleasantries had to be gone through first. Or maybe, just maybe, she was afraid to ask.

There was silence for a minute while the old woman negotiated a steep slope. Wambui put out a hand to give her some support. When the aunt had recovered her breath, Wambui asked, as casually as she could: "Tata, what news of Irungu?"

"Irungu will come tomorrow."

"He said that before, but still he never comes."

"He has been busy."

"What is it that keeps him so busy in Nairobi?"

"He will come tomorrow. He has more time now he's finished building—" She broke off, biting her lip.

Wambui felt as if she were choking. Her voice came out high-pitched and strangled. "What is Irungu building in the city? A house?"

"I was not supposed to tell you. Sorry."

"But how can you lie to me? How can you protect him?"

"Forgive me, child. It was not Irungu I was trying to protect."

They had reached the *shamba,* and Aunt Wairimu gathered back her belongings.

"Go, now, Wambui," she said gently. "Finish the planting before Irungu comes."

The child was waking now, so Wambui sat herself down under the banana tree. She unwound the cloth and brought the baby round to her lap, opening the buttons of her blouse and slipping her nipple into his mouth. His huge, dark eyes stared steadily at her as he suckled. She felt a fierce surge of love for the child and then a shudder of revulsion for Irungu. For the pretense. The lies.

What a fool she had been to imagine that her marriage was different from all the others! She knew the stories of so many girls in her position, and she had often participated in deluding these women—assuring them that their husbands were faithful, when everyone knew they weren't. All that time she, herself, was being deceived. And she had never suspected.

The first time Irungu came home from the city, driving that shining silver car, Wambui had been worried. He was dressed in a dark suit and tie and a gleaming white shirt. His leather shoes shone.

His mother, aunts, sisters, brothers, cousins, and neighbors had all gathered round, admiring him, admiring the Mercedes, where it was parked halfway up the lane. The little ones touched the car tentatively with their fingers and Irungu scolded them, making a big show of taking out a cloth and polishing off fingerprints. He told them that his boss would be very displeased if he found marks on his Mercedes. Being a driver was such a responsible job. Not only did he have to drive the boss to work and take the boss's wife shopping and his children to school, but he had to keep the car spotless. Wambui could see them all looking at him in awe. Every child among them was wishing he was grown up, so that he, too, could be a driver like Irungu.

And Wambui had felt proud, but troubled. Now that Irungu had this new job, he could come home only for a few days each month. He would be away in the city most times without her. And the city women would not be immune to his charms and his good looks, so enhanced by his new attire and by his job as driver of a Mercedes. She had caught sight of herself in the panel of the car, her body heavy and pregnant with Irungu's child. She had smoothed back her short hair, plaited into itself in a kind of zigzag pattern. She was conscious for the first time of how unsophisticated she must seem in his eyes.

Two weeks after the birth of his child, Irungu had come home again. Proudly, Wambui had placed the baby in his arms. "Look Irungu, your first-born. A boy-child."

The baby was perfect and beautiful. But it seemed that his joy at the birth of his son was muted. He was restless, impatient about the harvesting of the maize, anxious to be on his way back to the city. That night, he had lain beside her but remained preoccupied and distant. His body, usually insatiable, never stirred with desire for her.

Yes, of course she had known. But she had hidden that knowledge in some shadowy place in her mind, where it could not hurt her. She had deluded herself. Anger boiled inside her, not just against Irungu, but against herself, against Aunt Wairimu, and everyone else who had supported the lie.

They said a man could not last more than a few weeks without a woman. That was their nature. If it was only some woman from the streets he was dallying with, it would not be so bad. She would have expected that. But this woman had been favored over herself. Irungu had taken the money Wambui had earned—money that was promised for her new house—and had spent it on a house for another woman.

Of all the feelings churning through and through her mind, the strongest one was hatred for that woman. She took the feeling for a moment. Held it. The intensity of it frightened her.

Wambui pulled her hand into a fist and pounded the earth under the banana tree. It was the woman's face she saw. She punched the tree trunk; punched and punched, imagining the woman's body. A crimson stream of blood flowed across her fingers. She sucked the injured knuckle and realized it was her own blood she was tasting. But she did not care. The need to hurt was too great. She punched the tree again.

The child began to cry, disturbed by the movement and the agitation of the mother.

"Sorry, baby, sorry."

She moved him round to the other breast and forced her body to be still.

Wambui looked back at her straw house. Through the hole in the roof, a stream of smoke was rising from the fire that Aunt Wairimu had lit. The house stood defiantly. It goaded her. It insulted her by its existence. It was primitive. It was old. It was rickety. It leaked when it rained. It stank of decay. It was riddled with termites.

She hated that hut. Irungu had promised her a proper house. He had cheated her. First he had gone away and now he had built her house. Built it far away from here. Built it in the city. Built her house. Her stone house.

"I will not be treated like this!" she resolved. "First, I am going to burn down that heap of sticks that he expects me to live in. Then I will go to Nairobi and demand to live in my stone house."

But the plan was no sooner made than it was discarded. How could she go there? That woman would be there.

Wambui strapped the baby on to her back and went to finish her planting. She gave another look of disgust at the hut. And then she thought that if Irungu had built a house in Nairobi, that, at least, meant that he would not bring his other woman here. Thank God she would be spared the disgrace of that! Anyway, a city woman would not come here to live in a straw hut. A city woman would not dirty her hands in the clay of the *shamba*. City women wore fine clothes. They smoked cigarettes and drank beer. They bleached their faces and wore extensions in their hair. Wambui had seen them herself, on the few occasions she had been to Nairobi.

The planting was finished now. Wambui shouldered her *jembe* and trudged wearily back up the *shamba* to the house.

A smell of cooking wafted from the pot above the fire and Aunt Wairimu spooned mashed potato, maize and beans onto a plate. The old woman dandled the child on her lap while Wambui ate.

"I have left the chicken for tomorrow when Irungu comes," she said.

"He deserves nothing from me, or from you, either," Wambui complained.

"Ah, child," said Aunt Wairimu, sighing. "Always, it is like this in the beginning. But you will get used to it. Like I have."

"You, Auntie. Yes, I know. But I did not expect this. My parents have a Christian marriage. Why can't I?"

"Things are not always as they seem, Wambui. Somehow, we are caught between the old values and the new ones. People find much room for disregarding any rules that do not suit them."

Wambui nodded. She knew the truth of what her aunt said. Irungu might have made promises to the priest and the Christian god, but he would argue that those promises were made to the god of the white man and that his people had their own god and their own traditions.

In her heart she knew that those promises Irungu made meant nothing. He would believe in whatever belief suited him best.

Wambui lowered her head and let the tears fall from her. The aunt put her arm around her and Wambui looked up into her face.

"What will I do, Tata?"

"There is nothing to be done, Wambui."

The aunt turned from Wambui and concentrated on the baby on her lap, stroking his back gently to lull him to sleep. "You will always be the first wife, Wambui. Mother of his first-born son. It is not so very bad." Then the aunt half closed her eyes and began her story: "Long, long time ago, when the great Ngai was dividing the universe, he brought our father, Gikuyu, to these lands to be the first tiller of the soil. Then he created the mountain of brightness as a dwelling place for himself, so he could rest there when he came to inspect his territory.

"Gikuyu's wife, Moombi, gave birth to nine daughters. Gikuyu made sacrifice and raised his hands to the mountain of Kirinyaga. Ngai came to his assistance. 'Go down to the sacred fig tree,' Ngai told him, 'and there you will find nine handsome young men who will marry your daughters.' And so it was.

"Gikuyu's descendants were many in the next generations. The daughters of Moombi ruled over the world and over their menfolk. But the women became selfish and cruel. They took many husbands and, through spite and jealousy, they put their men to death, even for trivial offenses such as infidelity. No matter how the men pleaded with them for leniency, they would not bend their ears to listen.

"At that time, the women were very fierce fighters and were stronger than the men. And so the men came together and thought out a plan to free themselves. They all went home at the same time, and every man lay down with his woman. After six moons had passed, all the women were swollen with child and were helpless. The men rose up against them and won the world for themselves. And so it is that men have won the right to decide what is best for all of us."

"I do not believe that, Tata."

"You can believe or not believe. It is still part of what we are."

Late the next afternoon, Wambui saw the green and blue bus pull in at the stop below. Irungu jumped down the steps and waved up at her where she stood. She felt the rising pace of the blood in her veins and tried to quell any trace of joy she felt at seeing him. All that was over now.

As he made his way up the hill toward her, she watched him, wondering vaguely why he had traveled by bus instead of driving. Perhaps he did not want to be seen when he arrived, she thought, because of what he had to tell her.

When he approached, she saw that his handsome face had been damaged: the nose flattened and bent slightly to the left, a purple snake of scar twisting through his right eyebrow. She paused, in shock for a second. He caught her off-guard with his embrace. Already, she was holding his face away from her, surveying it, forgetting that this was not the same Irungu, her husband.

"What is this? What happened?"

His smile was radiant and unchanged. "Ah, that? It was an accident."

"The Mercedes?"

"It was not as lucky as I was."

She almost smiled, but remembered herself and drew her mouth into a tight, hard line.

"Wambui, what is wrong? Are you not glad to see your Irungu alive?"

"Yes, I am glad." It was the truth. She might wish his woman dead, but not Irungu.

He had turned his attention to the child now, and was making a great fuss of him, tickling him and holding him up in the air so that he laughed. And then Aunt Wairimu was waiting at the door and was ushering them in, serving up steaming bowls of chicken soup. It was not turning out at all as Wambui had planned.

After the meal, Aunt Wairimu went back to her own house, while the young couple went to inspect the *shamba*. It had rained a little overnight and the maize plants were looking pert and green.

"Take me to Nairobi," Wambui said. "Let me live in your new stone house."

Irungu looked steadily at her. There was no sign of guilt in his eyes. And then he laughed, a huge, merry laugh, and Wambui hoped in her heart that that meant it wasn't true.

"Ah, you have made a mistake! This shack that I built is so small, it would fit three times into our house."

"It is not made of stone?"

"Timber and tin."

That was some consolation at least. "How can you afford to buy land in Nairobi?"

"Ah, Wambui, what would you know about these things?" Again, he was laughing at her. "This land is squatters' land."

"You have built a house on someone else's land? Without permission?"

He shrugged. "That land was taken from the Kikuyu, anyway."

"So, you do not mind if any Kikuyu comes in here to live on your land?"

"Ah, Wambui, why are you so angry with me? It is a hard life in the city. These landlords are so corrupt. Even they do not own the lands for which they charge rent. How can I afford to pay these people?"

"And you have no job?"

"That *mzungu* was always ordering me around. 'Jackson, do this. Jackson, do that.' As if I was his boy. Tomorrow, I will find a better job."

"When will you take me to see your new house?"

"Why would you want to go there, Wambui? You hate the city. Remember the time you went to Peponi Road?" How typical it was of him to disarm her like this, by prodding at her sore point, reminding her of her shame.

She had gone once to visit her friend, Shiku, who lived in a rich suburb of Nairobi. The name *Peponi* meant "heaven" and for years Wambui had fantasized about the mansion in which Shiku lived. But Peponi Road turned out to be a formidable place, with all the gateways locked and shuttered. Wambui had peered through a tiny peephole in a huge, black gate. She had barely snatched an eyeful of what could be seen of the house behind, when the gruff voice of a watchman spoke beside her: "What do you want?" Wambui jumped in fright. She wasn't sure if he was watching her through another peephole that she couldn't see. She looked around cautiously.

"Is Mama Shiku home?"

"Mama is not here."

She had wanted to explain that she and Shiku were the same age and had been at school together. If he told Shiku who she was, she would be glad to see her. But the words would not form in Wambui's mouth. There was a sign on the gate: *Wabwa wakali.* She was terrified of dogs. Later, Irungu told her that people in Nairobi put these signs on their gates even when they had no dogs. The signs were intended to keep thieves out. But that was what she had felt like then—like a thief—someone who had no right to be in that place. Wambui had slunk away from there, sad and ashamed. She had never told Shiku about her visit.

Irungu was right. She hated the city. It was too crowded, too hot, too airless. The streets and the buildings were all very bewildering, from the wide city streets and the skyscrapers to the tiny filthy tracks and clustered shacks of the slums. And there were so many women to steal her husband.

"You are not allowed to take another wife."

"According to whom?"

"The priest. The Catholic Church."

"I see. It is this priest who is poisoning you against me, interfering in our lives as usual."

"This has nothing to do with the priest."

"But it is he who says I must have only one wife. Tell him that I will have as many wives as I like and that my marriages will be approved under the customary law."

"So there *is* another woman."

He was calmer now. "No, Wambui, there is only you. But there is a principle. I will not have any white man telling me what I must do."

The clouds suddenly disappeared from the mountain and the huge peaks rose up dazzling white and breathtaking. Wambui felt a chill of cold air from the snowy glaciers. It seemed Ngai never tired of playing this game of hide and peep. Just when she thought she had escaped him, he appeared to drag her back to the old ways. She imagined Ngai laughing at her and her modern pretensions. Her wish to be an only wife. Her hopes for a stone house with glass windows. Ha ha ha.

Irungu put his two hands on her shoulders and looked her full in the eyes. "You know me, Wambui. Your Irungu. Your husband. I will not cheat you."

So, this is how it will be, she thought. He will lie to me and I will pretend to believe him. I will not do as Aunt Wairimu does—traveling up and down to visit her husband and his other family. And, in time, perhaps I will come to believe him—or to forget what I know.

As quickly as it had appeared, the great mountain was lost again under the blanket of night. Wambui followed her husband back to the refuge of the circular straw house.

3

Irungu stood at the big double gates and pressed the bell. Behind him, the life of the street streamed on unabated, traffic chugging past, drifts of pedestrians walking by. Loud music and drumbeats blared out from a passing bus. "*Matatu? Matatu?*" the bus tout called. He was standing on the step, clinging to the roof-rack and squashing the people inside to make more room.

"*Si taki,*" Irungu replied, glad that he didn't need to cram in there with all those people, suffocating, bathed in sweat. Besides, even if he were going somewhere, he couldn't afford a *matatu*.

Again, he pressed heavily on the bell. Kept his finger there a long time. People in the bus queue opposite watched him idly. He rattled the chain and bent down to look through the tiny peephole. His eye met the watchman's eye peering out.

"Who's there?"

"Irungu Maina."

"What do you want?"

"I spoke to mama on the telephone. She needs a gardener . . ."

"Mama!" the watchman's voice shouted. "This gardener he want to speak to you, all right?"

"You can let him in," he heard the faint reply.

The padlock was undone and the gate opened a fraction. Irungu stepped in and the watchman secured the chain again. There was a manicured lawn that was nearly as big as his own *shamba*. He hoped the *mzungu* woman had a lawnmower. Deep flowerbeds ran along the edges of the paths. The house was almost the whole width of the site, long and squat, with orange roof tiles and ornate, iron grids on the windows and doors. Irungu let out a low whistle. He would be lucky to land a job in a place like this. Still, he caught a small smile twitching at the corners of his mouth. Maybe the spate of bad luck that had begun with the accident with the Mercedes was about to leave him. The white mama's voice on the telephone had been kind and encouraging. And, this morning, he had had news from Kishagi that Wambui had borne him a second child—a daughter.

"I'm Mrs O'Flaherty," the woman greeted him, shaking his hand.

"Mama Frahelty," he attempted, his tongue battling with these foreign R and L sounds.

She laughed. "Oh, this mama title makes me sound so old!"

"But you are young," he flattered her. She was, inso-

far as he could tell. He found white people's ages hard
to figure out.

"You're a diplomat."

"Well, I once was a driver for the Spanish ambassa-
dor," he bragged. Maybe he should not have said that.
Maybe she would check. He looked down at his toes
and noticed that they were dusty. His feet were callused
and his toenails buckled. For an instant he wished he
had dressed in an impeccable suit and shiny leather shoes.

But the mama's laugh rang out warm and throaty.
She thought he had made a joke; she wouldn't check.

"Do you enjoy gardening?" she asked him. "Do you
like plants?"

"I have worked as a gardener before," he answered.
"I have a letter of recommendation." He gave her the
note, watching anxiously as she scrutinized it. He hoped
the large, spidery scrawl wasn't too obviously his own.

The white mama brought him round the side of the
house and down steps. His rubber sandals were made of
old tires and their back slap against his heels seemed
loud in the stillness of the compound. For a little diver-
sion, he plucked some weeds out of a flowerbed as he
passed by.

The garden had been landscaped into four levels,
along the natural sweep of the land, from the front gates
down to the back fence in the valley behind. She paused,
indicating a large patch, sparsely planted with spiky grass.

"The lawn wouldn't grow under the trees here," she said. "The landlord had to have it replanted."

"This is Kikuyu grass," he answered. "The leaves of the jacaranda tree cannot kill this one."

"Is that what it's called," she asked, "keekuyu?"

"Same name as my tribe. Native to these highlands."

"It'll grow well, so."

They surveyed the bottom end of the garden, down more steps, which were flanked with a railing.

"Can you start tomorrow?"

He felt himself grin. "You will take me on?"

"If you want the job."

He hesitated for a moment, caught in the half-grin. "What salary?"

"Two thousand three-hundred."

"Two-five."

"I'm told two-three is reasonable."

He shrugged. "It is okay."

Each day, Irungu swept down the paths using a besom that he had made of twigs. He watered the whole garden and pulled up the persistent weeds. In the heat of the afternoon, he lit a fire in the pit that he had dug in the bottom corner and, lying under a bougainvillea, he whittled sticks, carving shapes of birds and animals as he watched the flames licking through the dead leaves.

Most afternoons, the woman sat outside on her patio, a book open in her lap.

"What book are you reading?" he asked.

She showed him the cover. "It's by an Irish writer."

"Have you read any African writers—Ngugi wa Thiongo? Chinua Achebe?"

"No." She tried, vainly, to repeat the names. He wrote them down for her. And a few days later, she was reading one of the books he had recommended.

"When I was at school, I had to hide this book," he told her. "It was banned."

"It's the same where I come from," she said. "All the best books get banned."

Once, when she came down the steps to where he was sprawled under the bougainvillea, he expected that she would criticize him, but "What's that you're carving?" was all she asked.

"A bird."

"I can see that. What kind of a bird?"

"A hornbill." He showed her the parrot-like beak. "These hide their females in a hollow tree and block up the entrance. They come back only to feed her until the young ones are old enough to fly."

The woman laughed, but her mouth turned down at the corners. "Sometimes I feel like that. Incarcerated."

He did not know exactly what she meant, but he sensed something of her sadness.

"Here," he said, offering her the carving.

"For me?" Her face and eyes glowed with pleasure. "Thank you, Jackson."

Irungu had never liked any of his employers, but this one was all right. Even the task of cutting all that grass with a slasher was not as arduous as he had thought. He caught himself whistling happily as he went about his work.

The end of the month fell on a Saturday and he picked up a couple of bottles of beer on his way home to the squatters' village where he lived. He kicked off his sandals and lay back comfortably on the bed, which was divided from the room by a blanket strung from a length of twine. He always felt secure and private in this corner. He was pleased with himself today, with the crisp new notes that lined his pocket. And the *mzungu* woman had added an extra two hundred bob as a "bonus." Using his teeth, he prized the cap off the bottle and felt the cold rush of liquid down his throat. He had learned to like his beer cold during his chauffeuring days. The boss always carried a cooler in the back with icy beer that made him shiver. If he were honest, he would have to admit it was the same beer that had caused the destruction of the Merc. But Irungu was rarely honest with himself. He liked to dream his life into little stories in which he was always the smart one, the winner, like the wily old hare in the stories of his childhood. The one who would always laugh last and hardest. He relaxed, basking in his good fortune. Then the sound of a woman's voice made him almost jump out of his skin.

"My husband, Irungu Maina. They said he was here."

"He is here," a child's voice answered.

Irungu stumbled from the bed, drew back the blanket and was confronted by the stony face of his wife, Wambui.

"You said I was the only one."

There was no point denying it, now. Not with the children here. He said nothing.

"I see I am not even the first."

"Ah, but these children are not mine, they are my wife's. Only that one is mine." He nodded toward a little boy of about a year old, who was being dandled on the lap of an eight-year-old girl.

"I am your wife."

"The marriage is legal," he countered. It sounded lame even to his own ears.

"And you spend money feeding children that are not yours. Where is their father?"

"I never asked who their fathers were."

There was a silence. He had not expected silence. He had thought she would shout or scream or hit him. But Wambui stood as if her legs were not fit to hold her up. Looking at her, he noticed the strain and the redness in her eyes. Her first-born was clinging tightly to her skirts, trying to hide himself as he looked fearfully up at his father. Irungu grabbed a stool and pushed it behind her before she could fall.

"*Chai*," he said urgently to the little girl, who added

hot water to the pot of tea already made with milk and sugar. She poured a cupful of the sweet strong brew and placed it in Wambui's hand.

"Out," he snarled at the children and they scurried away to the brightness outside, leaving Irungu alone with his first family. Into the stillness left by their departure came the sound of rasping, gasping breath.

Gently, Irungu untied the cloth from his wife's back and took into his arms the frail bundle that was his newborn daughter.

Strangely, his first thought was, what a fool he was to have attached his luck to something as fragile as this. But then, the labored breathing reached to something deep inside him and he recognized in this child his own flesh, his own life, his own urgency to live. And the child's need to live overcame all other thoughts and feelings he had. He held the baby to him, buried his face between her little shoulder and cheek, and let the tears fall from him.

"What is this?" he asked Wambui. "What is wrong?"

"What is wrong? What is wrong? You ask me what is wrong?" Her voice was rising to a crescendo, as if the anger he had expected was releasing itself now that the child had been taken from her back.

Wambui's hand was shaking as it held the cup. Irrelevantly, he noticed the flowers on the cup—pink and blue, some kind of foreign flowers that he had never seen in real life. There was a crack in the cup and the tea oozed through, making a brown stain on the cloth of her skirt. Her voice rose without words and turned into a dreadful wailing that filled up the hut.

"Shush," he said urgently. "Shush."

But the cry swelled, rose, and fell and rose again, filtering out through the small gaps between the timbers and the flattened tin cans that made the walls. Seeping out to the neighbors only inches away. He could sense, rather than see, the eyes of the children peering through the slits. He didn't like scenes like this. Didn't want the whole neighborhood involved in this private matter. "Shush, Wambui." His own voice hushed to a whisper as if to tone down the wailing that went on and on. Shut her up, just shut her up, just make her stop, just don't let the woman cry like that. Deep in the throat, a half-moan rising, rising to a high-pitched wail, all pervading. If he blocked his ears she would see, he couldn't let her see him doing that.

The child's struggle for breath continued. The little boy was sniveling now, upset by his mother's crying. Irungu crossed to her and put his hand on her shoulder. She shook him off. He placed the baby in her lap. As he stepped back he saw, out of the corner of his eye, a flash of pink and blue. The cup shattered as it hit him above the ear. Hot tea scalded his neck and shoulder. He fingered a sore and sticky patch in his hair where the cup had cut through the skin. With relief, he realized that the crying had stopped.

"You." Wambui spat on the floor at his feet. "You are the one who has brought death to all of us. This child has AIDS."

Irungu closed his eyes. If all the cups and vessels of the world had been thrown at him, they could not have cut as deeply as her words. As what they contained: hopelessness and contempt.

When he opened his eyes again, he found himself looking at a poster on the wall. It was a skeleton sitting on a toilet. He had brought the picture home one time and he and Maria had shared a good laugh. Suddenly, the joke was too sick, too close.

He put his hand in his pocket and pulled out all of the crisp new notes.

"Take her to a hospital," he said. "Pay for anything she needs."

Wambui took the money and put it in her basket.

"No," he said. "Hide it. You will be robbed."

She slipped the money down inside her blouse.

"That is better."

She retied the baby on her back. Irungu picked up the little boy and wordlessly they left the hut. The children outside stared at them, big-eyed.

"Say nothing about this, you hear?" Irungu barked at them, as they slunk away.

He turned back to see the accusation in his wife's eyes. Not hurt. No hurt now. Past hurt. That stung him.

"How can it all be my fault, how can it?" he parried her wordless accusation.

She didn't answer. Funny, he had not expected her to. The eyes that looked back at him were cold. Dark. Without affection. Without love. He suddenly realized how much that meant. How empty he was, bereft of her love.

This was just something I drifted into, he wanted to say. Not anything like I had with you. I needed no other love but yours. But all those words were pointless now. It was all destroyed now. Destroyed by something he couldn't quite face or dare to name, although she had said the word. But though she had named the destroyer, it wasn't *it* she was blaming, it was him.

"This is so unfair," he muttered, "so unfair."

They followed the track through the lines of shacks that leaned and straggled into each other. Workers were making their way home now in noisy bunches, filled with payday elation and beer. They moved slowly against the crowd. The child, bewildered, hid his face in his father's shoulder. Irungu hugged him closer to put him at ease. They walked all the way to the bus station. The *matatus* were too jammed full and airless for them to travel with the baby.

Irungu waited with them until the bus came. No word was spoken. As Wambui took the child's hand and turned to go aboard, Irungu stroked his little daughter's head a last time.

***

When she passed away, six weeks later, Irungu asked his employer for a salary advance. There was some business up country he had to attend to, he told her. This was something he couldn't share with her. He couldn't bear her sympathy or her prying into the cause of death.

When he arrived in Kishagi, his hut was full of people. The priest was among them, sitting on a stool. What is he doing here? Irungu wondered as he got up and came toward him, his hand outstretched.

"I'm very sorry, Irungu. The only consolation is that she's with God."

"With the ancestors," Irungu snapped, aware suddenly of the quietness into which he spoke. Disapproving eyes looked at him from all quarters. He had forgotten that this religious stuff went with the death of a child. Somehow, he had thought of it as a purely personal thing. And it angered him—all these people jostling in like this into his grief, into his business, into his family. He caught a glimpse of Wambui glaring at him from the other side of the room. That quieted him. He had been about to order them all out of his house.

Nobody offered him a cup of tea or a bit of food after his journey. It was as if his coming was a signal for them all to start milling round. Or maybe they were trying to pre-empt his anticipated order to remove themselves from his home.

"Do you want to see her?" He became aware of the priest, still beside him.

"What?"

"Before we close the coffin." He nodded toward the small box that had been hidden by the crowd.

"See her? No." He remembered the last touch. It was what he wanted to remember.

"Right, so." The priest raised his hand and someone closed the clasps on the coffin. Before he knew it, Irungu, with his brothers, was shouldering the box at the head of a procession and was being nudged toward the village and the church.

Why should the box be white? something inside him asked, angry. Why white, why a priest, why a white man, why a church, why wasn't I asked?

The box was taken from him and placed on the steps at the foot of the altar. He was ushered into the front seat beside Wambui. She still hadn't greeted him. As the people crammed in, he was pushed against her and felt her stiffen. He thought of the time when the child had been conceived. How soft and voluptuous her body had been. That moment was so far away and unreachable now. Was it that night, that moment, that *it* had found its way through him into her and into the innocent young life that was forming itself inside her? *It.* He still hadn't found himself able to utter the word. To come to grips with what had happened. He was inarticulate when it came to these things. He didn't know how this disease worked, how it came or went or why. The priest was talking about God's will. Irungu wasn't really listening.

Let his own thoughts have their sway. He hoped Wambui hadn't told anyone. He was about to prod her in the ribs, to whisper to her, "Hey, Wambui, don't tell anyone. Don't tell—" when he heard the word in the mouth of the priest. AIDS.

Irungu's head shot up and he looked directly into the eyes of the priest. The blue eyes looked back at him, warm and moist with emotion.

"What we see here is only a tiny fraction of what there is. This disease is epidemic. I've heard it said that God has sent it as a judgement against the sexual practices of the people. But my God is not a god of vengeance, he is a god of love. He did not send this to Irungu and his family to punish them . . ."

Irungu heard no more. He could feel the eyes of the congregation turned on him. It had been named—AIDS. And he had been named as a carrier of it. He bundled some money out of his pocket and pushed it into Wambui's hand. He felt her fingers tighten round it. Then he stood up and shouldered his way out of the church. When he reached the highway, he flagged down a bus.

He lost himself then. Steeped in beer and *changa'a*, he woke in the mornings not knowing where or how he had slept. In the anonymity of the city, nobody knew what had befallen him, or that he was unclean. He thought about it that way sometimes. Like leprosy. But it didn't show like leprosy. He found women, even, who didn't know or didn't care. He lost himself in them. And the pain came back whenever he was sober and alone, so he tried never to be sober or on his own. Until he woke up one morning lying by the side of the road, irretrievably sober, his pockets empty, his money spent or robbed, he didn't know which. Even his sandals were gone. He drew in his aching legs and forced his body into a standing position.

Up the road, there was a man selling newspapers. "What day is it?"

"Sunday."

"What week, what month?"

"Ah," a grin spread across the newsboy's face. "You have been lost."

"Yes." Irungu grinned back at him.

"February twenty-first. How long?"

"Two and a half weeks."

"It must have been good *changa'a*."

"The best."

Irungu tried to put days and weeks into perspective but they were all the same, it seemed. Then, out of the haze, one memory slowly emerged and clarified itself, until it became as clear as the pure drop forming in the *changa'a* maker's still.

He was in the house of a small, fat man who must have been rich, judging by the stone house, the man's suit and tie and the television set blinking in the corner. On the table was a bottle of the illicit liquor which he poured copiously into two thick glass tumblers. This was a man with opinions that impressed Irungu greatly.

They had just watched a TV faith healer praying over a sick woman. His friend leaned toward Irungu and his voice boomed out loud and important. "You know this disease, this AIDS," he said and poked a large finger almost into Irungu's face.

"Yes." Irungu felt himself squirm.

"It was introduced by Europeans in a plot to cull the African people."

As this memory asserted itself, Irungu felt a huge burden lift from his shoulders. He felt absolved of all responsibility and guilt. Guilt was something foreign to his nature anyway—all part of the white man's religion. He had been proved right. None of this was his fault; he was the hapless victim of a conspiracy against himself and his people.

He found his way to a telephone box and tapped in his employer's number.

"This is Irungu Maina. My business is finished and I will be back tomorrow."

"I hope your trip was successful."

"Oh, yes, it was a great success." His words came bubbling out, full of exuberance. "There was an old dispute that I needed to settle. And I won."

4

The white woman answered the gate when the bell rang.

"Who is it?" she called, peering out through the peep-hole.

"It is me. Irungu."

"Who?"

"Jackson."

"Ah, you're back! Welcome." She swung the gate open and shook his hand. "Wait 'til you see your Kikuyu grass."

She brought him round the side of the house and showed him the little spiky plants. They had sprouted side-shoots that had filled up the spaces between. The grass had grown thick and green and shiny.

"Ir-oongoo," she said. "Is that what you like to be called?"

"Irungu," he corrected her. "It is my own name."

"Why the Jackson then?"

"The missionaries say we must put a Christian name before our own name."

She was surprised at the irritation in his voice. Remembering his phone call, she thought he had sounded different then, too. His voice had been high-pitched, and she had noticed that his words had tumbled out of him in a great gush of excitement.

"I'm glad," she said, "that your trip up country was such a success. And I'm glad you're back, too." She giggled. "I couldn't manage the slasher." The woman's voice faltered in the intensity of his silence. "Who will tend to your land, up country, while you're here?" she continued, hoping to break through whatever barrier had suddenly appeared between them.

"A woman will do that work."

Again she was stalled by the unexpected resentment in his voice.

The gate bell jangled and the gardener went and undid the lock on the front gates. A white car purred into the driveway and a fat Indian disengaged himself from the front seat. He whisked round the side of the house in a cloud of spicy aftershave and cigar smoke.

"Hello, madam. Everything fine? Good. I have brought you the bill for electricity."

"Would you like a cup of tea?"

"No. I am a busy man. What is your gardener called?"

"Jackson."

"Jackson!" he roared. "*Kuja hapa!*" Irungu came running up. "You, boy. Why you not cut this grass? Lazy boy. You sleep all day, no work. You *kata* now, d'you hear?"

After he was gone, the stink of his aftershave remained. The gardener came up beside the patio, shirtless, with the slasher in his hand.

She stepped down and crossed the lawn to him and touched his arm. "Irungu, it will do tomorrow."

He shook her hand away and kept going at the Kikuyu grass: the slasher flicking rhythmically up and over his shoulder in a neat arc, down again and around, bits of grass flying away over his head, rivulets of sweat running down his bare neck and chest.

She liked to sit with her books on the patio in the afternoons. But today, the gardener's mood seemed to detract from her pleasure. So she moved her chair around to the front garden where she would not have to watch him.

Next day she was glad that the grass was cut and that she could reclaim her patio. From here, she was parallel with the tops of the trees at the lowest level of the garden: ancient trees that were part of the original forests.

Sometimes, a squirrel would scurry along the fence and stop, sitting upright, looking around before continuing his foraging. There was no need for the squirrels here to hoard up food for the winter. In a land of two growing seasons, nature never slept.

The house girl tiptoed out to the patio. "Mama," she said, "this Kikuyu, he no eat *chakula*." She was almost in tears. "He throw it down. He say I no cook no more *chakula* from him."

He was lying under the bougainvillea and took his time responding to her call. She stood on the steps looking down at him. Called again. He stirred, sat up, plucked a blade of grass, got up slowly and climbed the steps to sit opposite her on the balustrade.

"What's this about your lunch?"

"I cannot have this person cook my food," he said. "She is a Nubian woman. Muslim. Unclean."

"Mariam always keeps herself clean."

"You do not understand," he said. "It makes my stomach sick to have my food touched by someone like that. I cannot eat it. Pah!" He spat out the blade of grass he had been chewing.

Next day, she cooked his maize and beans herself. But the beans took hours on the gas cooker and were constantly needing attention. Why am I doing this? she asked herself. I would rather be gardening than cooking for the gardener.

They agreed that he would go to the kiosk for his lunch. She paid the money in advance. Two hundred bob per week. It seemed a fair compromise.

Irungu turned the padlock to the front and put the key in his pocket when he went to the kiosk for lunch. The woman was glad of this private hour to sunbathe. She expected that he would ring the bell when he came back. She did not hear him as he let himself in. She had dragged the sun bed out into the middle of the grass and was lying there almost naked.

Looking up suddenly, she saw him standing there. He turned away, a look of disgust on his face. Hastily, she retrieved her clothes and retreated into the house. When she came outside again, he was working in the flowerbed. "Irungu, I read that your people had tally sticks put around their necks and that, every time they spoke Kikuyu, a notch was put in the stick. You know, the same was done to us when we spoke Irish."

He dug the fork into the soil and with an irritated movement, poked a weed out of the flowerbed.

Later, she approached him again. "I'm sorry if I embarrassed you earlier."

"A white woman's body does not interest me," he said. "It has no color; it has no shape. Why do you think I should be embarrassed?"

"But, Irungu—"

"Do not call me by that name."

Some time later, she passed by and he was still weeding. He didn't look up as she stopped beside him. "I'm new here," she told him. "I haven't yet learned the ways of your country."

He stood up and swiveled round to face her. "Why do you keep interrupting me?" The weeding fork was in his hand. He let it drop and it clattered on the path. "If I do that once," he said, "you will say I am careless." He bent down and picked up the fork. Then, watching her, he slowly dropped it again. It was louder this time, as it clanged on the ground. "If I do it twice, you will say I am foolish." He reached down and scooped up the fork again. Then he dashed it down hard. It rattled across the path and hit the wall of the house. "If I do it three times, you know I am deliberately trying to distract you."

"Where I come from, we're always talking," she said. "If a man comes in to do a job in the garden, he says hello every time he passes by the window. That's just our nature."

The long rains came. Flights of white ants descended like huge snowdrifts, landing on the lawns, on the patio, seeping in, somehow, through locked windows, under doors, through keyholes. In the morning, all that was left was their white, discarded wings. Beautiful, lost. The gardener was kept busy with his sweeping.

She was sitting on the patio when he called her out. "Mama, I want you to see something. Close the doors."

She slid the patio doors shut and followed him down to the steps.

There he turned and looked back, pointing. "Tell me what you see in the windows."

"Reflections of the garden."

"Can you see through them? Can you see inside?"

"No, I can't."

He shrugged and walked away from her.

The rain came pelting down, churning up the earth in the beds around the house, splashing red soil up the walls. She padlocked the iron grilles on the patio, padlocked the iron gates on the front doors. Darkness had fallen at half-past six. She lay in bed listening to the sounds of the night. Crickets chirped. A bushbaby laughed in a tree outside her room. She hopped out of bed and squinted out through the iron bars of the window. They were creatures with big moon-shaped faces, she knew, but she had never managed to glimpse one. All she saw now was the darkness and the deeper shadows of the trees. The sound of the mocking laughter rang out again across the garden.

She curled back into bed and listened for the steady tread of the night watchman as he patrolled the compound. Then the rain came again, heavy, relentless. There would be no more reassuring footsteps round the house tonight. The *askari* would not move from his warm stove and his sentry box.

In the morning, the air was stultifying; the clouds were full and threatening. An ache in her head told her there was thunder somewhere, not too distant. Irungu had not come to work. She paced in and out of the house, unable to settle on the patio or with her books.

The *dring, dring* of the telephone made her jump.

"Hello?"

"This is the police."

"Yes."

"This man here, he say he is *shamba* boy for you. You will speak with him?"

"I will."

"It is me. Jackson."

"Are you all right?"

"They want a chit, to say I am employed by you."

"I'll bring it."

She took out the original contract she had signed with him and a copy of his identity card, bearing his photograph and the stamp of his thumbprint.

The police station was an old colonial building, long and low, in cut stone. Wet mud had been churned up from the pathways and walked through by countless feet, creating a red trail up the steps and into the barracks.

People in the waiting room went quiet and stared at her. She was the only white person there. Sometimes, she wished she could hide her face with a veil, the way the coastal women did, disguise herself so no one would know she was different. The policeman behind the counter ignored her. A woman moved and made space on the bench. Smiling thanks, she squeezed in beside her.

A man came out from inside and signaled her. "Madam." The hinged section of the counter was raised and she was ushered through to an adjoining room.

"What can I do for you, madam?"

He was a tall, gaunt man with skin much darker than Jackson's was. He turned the document over in his hands. "I do not think this is enough," he declared. "How do I know you are this person?"

"I have my driver's license," she said, opening her purse and searching through the pockets. His eyes lighted on the obvious bundle of notes in her purse.

"I do not think this is enough," he said, turning the driver's license in his hand.

Cursing that she had nothing smaller, she placed a five-hundred-shilling note on the desk.

She heard the rattle of keys and the squeal of the cell gate, the resounding clank of steel closing on steel and the rattle of keys again. "He can go with you now, madam."

Irungu kept his eyes downcast as they went out to the car. When she sat into the Land Rover and leaned across to open the door for him, he climbed wordlessly up into the passenger seat.

"Did they beat you?" she asked.

Irungu didn't answer her, but the expression on his face and the deep red color in his eyes told her what he would not tell.

She handed him the contract document. "You'd better make a copy of this," she said, "for the next time."

He took the paper from her, folded it carefully, then tore it to shreds. The pieces fell to the floor of the car. She revved the engine and drove out of the yard.

"It is not this they want," he said suddenly. "I had a hundred shillings in my pocket. I would not pay a bribe."

They passed the monument to independence—a giant hand clasping a ceremonial stick.

"They took it anyway," he said.

"Took what?"

"My hundred bob."

She stopped at the lane that led down to the slum

village where he lived. He banged the car door and she watched his small, abject figure as he picked his steps down the uneven path. Beyond him, acres of tin and straw roofs spread out higgledy-piggledy, like mushrooms trying to squeeze each other out, jostling for space. Vivid blue forks of lightning sizzled through the black clouds as she moved off. Fat raindrops tumbled out of the sky.

The coolness brought by the rains remained after they were gone. There was no sunshine. She wore her cardigan when she sat outside.

From her patio she noticed a tiny movement, green against green. She approached on tiptoes the enormous split leaves of the monstera plant. And there it was: eyes swiveling in opposite directions, three little horns on the tip of its nose, scaly skin—a chameleon. The front right and the back left feet moved in perfect unison, a hesitant double-step forward, clinging to the leaf as the front left and the back right were released in another staggered two-step.

She placed her hand in the creature's path. The little eyes kept swiveling; the rhythm never stopped. Release, half-step, hold; the right foot caught on her hand. Release, half-step, hold; three of the four legs were on her palm. Its skin began to lose its greenness, becoming translucent. She lifted her hand and laid it down in the soil at the base of the plant. The chameleon never faltered. It marched off into the flowerbed and its skin, slowly, slowly, changed to brown.

"You should not touch that one. It is bad."

"Look, Jackson! It's beautiful." She picked the chameleon up on her hand again. "It has no color of its own, see?" She moved it up from the soil to the leaf and down again. "The color is only a reflection of where it is."

He backed away from her, horrified. "Even the elephant fears that one," he said.

She sat fewer days outside now; it was too gloomy, too cold. The clouds seemed to have lodged above the treetops, trapping the pollution in the air above the city. Diesel fumes from the road seeped into the garden. Jacaranda leaves separated into their tiny feathery leaves and showered down on the lawn.

"I am a man," Jackson told her, "I have a wife, I have children. In my tribe I am respected."

"Yes, I know that."

"Why do you treat me like a small boy?"

"I have always treated you with respect."

Whenever she went outside, he seemed to be waiting with another accusation.

"You're racist," he challenged her.

She folded her book over slowly in her lap. "No. It's you who are racist. You're blaming me for wrongs that other white people have done to your people. The Irish were colonized, too, and they carry the same grudges."

He took to hanging around the patio waiting for her to appear. She took to reading in the sitting room with the door closed.

From inside, she watched his restless roaming through the garden. He was always on this level now, passing by the windows, peering in. Day after day he paced, his brow puckered in a permanent frown. Weeds invaded the Kikuyu grass.

She left him alone. Maybe when the sun shone again and the blossoms burst out on the jacaranda, he would come back to himself.

"Mama, nice carrots, nice price." "Avocados, Mama, avocados." "Mama, roses." "Oranges, Mama, you promise." "Mama, Mama, you my customer." She was surrounded after she came out of the supermarket. "Mama, Mama, Mama." They all babbled together, pushing their produce into her face.

"No." She tried to wave them off: "*Si taki, si taki,* I don't want."

The boy from the supermarket carried her groceries and when she opened the car door, the traders piled their fruits, vegetables, and flowers in beside the bags. She paid the boy his tip. The sales pitch increased, everyone talking at once. She knew she could not get away without buying something. It was always the same. She often ended up with more carrots and oranges than she could eat, and at twice the price of the supermarket.

"What are you selling, Mama?" she asked a wizened old woman on the edge of the crowd. A black, earthenware pot was presented in answer.

"This mama know no white language," said the man with the oranges. "Me, I will help you."

Most of the others slunk away, muttering. A few remained to help the old mama make a good price.

She had been fleeced, she knew. The same pots were available in the market for a fraction of the cost. But they were lovely, black and round-bottomed. She pulled into the gateway and beeped the horn for Irungu to come and let her in.

"Look what I bought," she said, opening up the boot. "Will you fill these for me, please, while I go to the nursery to get some flowers?"

"Flowers, flowers," she heard him mutter as he picked up a pot. Then he turned around and said: "Do you know how many families could be fed from a piece of land this size?"

Although disquieted, she tried to laugh it off. "I can imagine the landlord's reaction if I turned his garden into a farm!"

He turned away from her and carried the pots down to the bottom of the garden. She watched as he took his machete and sliced a square of ground. Then he broke up the soil with the blade of the hoe and, using his hands, started to scoop the soil into the pots.

When she returned from the nursery, he did not answer the gate. Eventually, it was the house girl who responded to her frantic beeping of the car horn.

She found the gardener sitting cross-legged on the patio. In his lap was one of her new earthenware pots.

"Irungu!" Her voice had a shrill edge to it as she slid back the sitting room door. She unhooked the lock on the iron grilles and flung them open. "Jackson! Why didn't you answer the gate?" She could feel her face flushing crimson. "You kept me waiting twenty minutes," she said. "I could have been murdered in my own gateway! What were you doing?"

For the first time, she noticed the tin of white gloss paint open beside him. Even as she watched, he calmly lifted a paintbrush, dripping white, and daubed the flowerpot. The paint spread out over the black surface, claiming more and more of it.

She stepped out on the patio. Three more round-bottomed pots were lined up. They had all been painted white. "Christ Almighty! What have you done to my pots?"

"It is not good," he said, "for a black African pot to sit on a white woman's patio in the Kikuyu highlands."

"You don't leave this place this evening," she shouted, "until every speck of that paint is cleaned off." She marched down the steps. "And I want every single weed removed from this lawn. Now! D'you hear me?"

"I'm not deaf."

Seeing him, suddenly, she stopped. She looked at the defaced pots; looked back at the gardener. A machete was lying at his feet. Beside it lay the hoe, heavy bladed, lethal. "Jesus!"

He had put the pot down and was slowly rising to

his feet. She ran up the steps, sidled past him, and fled into the house. Her fingers trembled as she secured the lock on the door.

The gardener looked in at her, a big, knowing smile on his face. "See," he said, "I told you you were a racist. You're just the same as all the others."

Leaning her hot forehead against the cool wall of the bedroom, she pressed the security button.

Two minutes later, a van pulled in and the gardener sauntered out to answer the gate. Six helmeted *askaris* jumped out, their truncheons drawn. Only then did she go outside.

"I want you to escort this man from my premises," she said. She handed him a bundle of money. "Three months' salary in lieu." For an instant, she wondered if he would throw it at her feet, or shred it. Or say something. But he counted the notes and shoved them into his pocket as he was led away.

5

It was that quiet hour of evening in Kishagi. I was outside on my veranda, in my favorite place, surrounded by warm darkness. Only the scratch of crickets, the screech of a cock, and the occasional bark of a dog broke the calm. Lights were on in the sacristan's compound next door and I noticed a white Peugeot that was drawn up beside the house. Nicolas' daughter, Shiku, was home on one of her visits. Yes, I remembered, Nicolas had mentioned it when he had brought me my newspaper and some post that he had collected from the PO box. I moved my chair to beneath my patio light, so I could read the paper. And there I sat, relaxing, scanning the news, procrastinating. One of the letters looked ominous. I had recognized it immediately by its Episcopal seal. I ignored it for a while, until I had digested everything that was digestible, and a lot that was indigestible, in the newspaper. No matter how many years I had lived here, I could never reconcile myself to the suffering, the heartbreak, the conflict, the disasters that were written out in such excruciating detail in the papers. With a sigh, I turned to the letter in my lap and broke the seal.

It read:

Dear Father O'Sullivan,

Reports have reached me and are causing me grave concern. It appears that you are continuing to ignore my instructions regarding your role as priest in Kishagi. I wish to warn you that these violations of the rule of obedience will not be tolerated. What you are doing is an embarrassment to me, personally, and to our Holy Father in Rome.

The deacon, John Kariuki, has reported that you preached a message from the pulpit, advocating the use of contraceptive devices. Let me remind you that the use of contraception is strictly prohibited under the laws of the Church. Your behavior is unacceptable. Your colleague, John Kariuki, was at the forefront of the rally that burnt these offensive rubber articles in the streets, at the time of the Papal visit. I was disap-

pointed, then, that you did not show
solidarity with our campaign. But,
now, it has become obvious that you
were deliberately flouting my author-
ity in this matter.

Even more seriously, I am told
that you have taken a political
stance on land issues in the Kishagi
area. Again, from the pulpit, I believe that you mentioned the name of
a leading politician and suggested
that he was involved in an intrigue
to defraud the people of what was
rightfully theirs. Let me remind you,
Father O'Sullivan, that political
wrangles are beyond your brief. It is
not the duty of a priest to defend
property but to deal with the spiritual needs of his flock and direct
them to their true home which the
Lord has prepared for them in Heaven.
Political involvement by a man of the
cloth is absolutely foolhardy in a
country such as ours, where we are
dependent on the ruling party for
permission to conduct our affairs. If
you persist with this, I will have
you removed from your parish and from
the country."

I crumpled up the letter and shoved it into my pocket. Damn. Damn. Damn. After a few minutes pacing and calming myself, I found a reply formulating itself in my head. I went inside to my desk, pulled out a clean sheet of paper, took up my pen and wrote:

Your Grace,

Since the visit of our Holy Father, the AIDS crisis has worsened considerably. Every week I bury young children and young mothers. Babies are born with AIDS. The entire fabric of the community in which I am working is crumbling. I am not advocating the use of condoms as a contraceptive device, rather as a means of preserving life—the lives of our children and our young people, who are the future of our Church. No missionary with a heart can stand idly by and allow his parishioners to be decimated by this avoidable disease. The deacon, John Kariuki, believes that it is a punishment sent by God to make our people alter their sexual behavior. I do not believe that God is such a monster. I believe He is a god of love

I had paused, considering, praying, I think, when the front door burst open. I heard it bang back violently against the wall.

"Hold on," I called, looking up, presuming it was an emergency. A sick call. Somebody needing the Last Rites.

A gang of men jostled into the room. Six or seven of them, maybe. They were making plenty of noise. There was no stealth involved. I got up from my desk. Turned to greet them. Saw him—the one with the *panga*. Saw him raise it. Saw it fall. Felt the thrust of it as it went through me. Felt the stab and then the slice downward. Found myself looking into his eyes. A face? No. No face. Covered, maybe. Yes, a cloth covered the face. Just the eyes showed. Eyes full of hatred. He meant to kill me. That was a horrible realization. What could I ever have done to anyone to make them hate me like that?

I have no memory of them after that. Whether they turned the place over, stole anything, stayed, went, I don't know. All I knew was my own pain. The struggle inside me—first against pain and, gradually, against the knowledge that I was mortally wounded.

I saw myself as a boy. Felt again the stirrings of that great mission, that great adventure that had set me apart from my peers, apart from my family. Felt suddenly the waste of it. This awful closure of a life unfinished, un-fulfilled, without the blessing of a son or the comfort of a woman to hold me or to mourn my passing. Saw the face of my father. Understood something of the barrenness of his dying. The presence there of a celibate son. Felt, like another stab wound, my own emptiness in dying childless.

And there was panic along with severe pain. It can't be. I can't die. Not now. Not like this. Not here. Not without a child. And the waves of pain wracked my body, running through and through.

I think I screamed. Maybe no sound came but I screamed. Think I screamed. And then I knew for definite that I was dying. But, by now, the pain was unbearable; I couldn't breathe. I stopped wanting to hold on. Started to move willingly toward release, toward cessation of pain.

And then I was completely alone, cut off from the possibility of ever relating to anyone. A wave of sorrow engulfed me for the life I hadn't lived. It is too late now, I told myself, and allowed the pain to wash over me, take me out with it like a tide and swamp me. I didn't struggle. I was only glad that it would end. That soon there would be no more pain.

My final thought was that if, by any miracle, I survived, I would have to go through all of this again.

I let go and found myself falling, falling beyond pain, beyond living, into absolute calm. There wasn't even a sense of having reached anything or any place. Just this wonderful, unearthly peace.

There were no trumpets, no angels, no tunnels, no face of God, no gates. I didn't hover above myself. I just died and found absolute peace. Eternal peace.

6

His papers were still scattered on the table where he had left them. They seemed undisturbed, Shiku noticed, as she gathered them together into a bundle. She picked his chair up from the ground where it had been flung back in those last minutes of terror. What thoughts must have gone through his mind when he realized that they had come for him? Poor Ciarán. Poor, credulous Ciarán, persistently seeing good in everyone, no matter how much anyone tried to warn him. Ciarán was a man unlike any other she had met. Unworldly. Otherworldly perhaps—living to the laws of his god, not frightened by the doings of men. Well, they had done for him this time. It was over. The dark pool of his blood was drying already, soaking into the concrete floor. A cloud of mosquitoes shimmered above the huge red stain. She felt a stab of pity for the man whose life had ebbed away there, just now, in this house. Poor fool. Then, another feeling welled up in her, unbidden. Deeper than pity. A wrench, somewhere round or about her heart and through her stomach. "No," she said, stifling that forbidden, half-forgotten emotion, but tears came scalding to her eyes.

A sound outside in the darkness made her jump. She took the notebooks and papers quickly and hid them inside her blouse. He might have written something that could be used in evidence against him, she thought. She should keep these safe. Perhaps she would send them to his mother in Ireland. The papers were coarse and scratchy against her skin. She hugged them tighter to herself. They were all that was left now of Ciarán's life.

Shiku slipped quietly out the back door, unlocked as always. How many times had her father lectured Ciarán about locking doors? But he would not listen.

"What," he would ask, "if someone needed me in the middle of the night?"

"What," her father would answer, "if someone came to rob you?"

Ciarán would shrug and open his hands in an expansive gesture. "If they need to rob me, then their need is greater than mine."

She hesitated at the bottom of the veranda steps, peering fearfully around her, waiting for her eyes to become accustomed to the darkness. One of the intruders might still be hiding in the compound. She listened intently. The only sounds that came to her ears were the never-ending hum and chirp of insects, the scratch and cluck of a hen as it settled in the hen house and, farther off, the bark of a dog.

She crept forward toward the orchard. Something brushed against her. Shiku screamed and fought as the thing caught and tangled in her hair. She clawed herself free and cowered down behind the broad trunk of an avocado tree. Peering fearfully out, she strained to see what it was that had assailed her. It was no living thing, she knew. She could still feel it on her face, dry and hard and scratchy. Then she sobbed a half-laugh, half-cry, as she recognized what it was: an old, discarded snake skin, hanging harmlessly down from the branch of a tree. The snake was long gone, slithered off in its shiny new-grown skin—the remnants of its former life left dry and abandoned.

Shiku could make out all of the compound now: the trees of the orchard, the outbuildings, the hen house, the perimeter fence, and, silhouetted black against the blue-black sky, the crucifix on the roof of the church in the compound next door. Nothing stirred.

She clutched her arms around herself and her precious bundle and sidled over to the gap in the wooden fence—left unmended since she was a teenager. Over the years, Shiku's father had become as lax about his caretaking as Ciarán was about matters of security.

"Wanjiku? Is it you?"

"Yes, Mama."

Her mother cranked open the big key, so rarely closed in the lock, and her face peered out, red-eyed. "Have you seen your father?"

"He has taken Father Ciarán in my car. They are gone to the airstrip to meet the doctors."

Her mother blessed herself and relocked the door. "Maybe they will save him."

"It is too late, Mama. I heard him scream. It was the death scream."

"Did they steal anything? Did they damage the church?"

"Nothing was touched."

Shiku said goodnight to her mother and went into her own room where she could be alone with her thoughts, her feelings, her memories.

When Father Ciarán first came to Kishagi fifteen years before, she was just fourteen. He must have been around the same age, then, or younger than she was now. He had told her it was his first parish. All he had ever wanted, since he was a small boy, was to come and work in a parish in Africa. When he had arrived in the village, the church bell was ringing and that was a sign that he had found the right place. Kishagi, he said, was in the middle of the world, between the north and south.

He was such a change from the gray-haired old man who had been his predecessor. Through their teens, Shiku, Wambui, and Irungu had visited his house regularly. They were always made welcome and the fridge was well stocked with treats, which she presumed he must have bought especially for them, as he never seemed to take any of them himself. The priest's house had the only electricity generator in the village at that time, and he had a record player and tape recorder. He had a bundle of old records from the 'sixties and 'seventies. She had learned to know and sing so many songs by the Beatles, Simon and Garfunkel, Neil Young. Wambui and Irungu were more interested in what they called their "own" music. They brought in tapes and danced to them in his kitchen.

Wambui, in those days, was always at Shiku's side. They were age-mates. Inseparable. And everywhere Wambui went, Irungu followed. He had never been as impressed by Father Ciarán as the girls were.

"Kilani is just the same as the rest of them," Irungu said. "A neo-colonialist."

"Neo-what?" Shiku laughed. "Irungu, you read too many of those political books. Would you like Father Ciarán better if he was an African priest?"

"I do not like any priest, but especially a white priest."

"How can you say that? He has done so much in the two years that he has been here. Look at the water scheme. What about the new generator that is being built?"

"The elders did that. Not Kilani."

Irungu's disloyalty bothered Shiku. It was so unfair of him to sit there in a man's kitchen, listening to his stereo, drinking his soda and criticizing him—not to his face, though. Never to his face.

"See it your own way. I think the man is like magic."

"That is because you fancy him. You do."

"How can I fancy a priest?"

But what Irungu said was true. She was infatuated with him. He seemed so vibrant, so full of life, so full of ideas. And the thought of him as a virgin at that age—a grown man who had never been with a woman—seemed so unnatural to her. Wambui and Irungu were already together at that stage. They would hold each other close, lie together but never fully naked. Irungu knew his pleasure and he took it when he could. They were like a wise, old, experienced couple in comparison to her. She began to tease Ciarán—wiggled her hips whenever she knew he was watching, brushed her hand against his, sometimes, to see the pink color spring into his cheeks.

But there were other reasons for her fascination. She was impressed by the fact that he was an outsider who had seen other parts of the great big world out there. From the moment she had met Ciarán, there was never any possibility that her life would be spent in Kishagi. He had opened her up to worlds beyond. And her favorite place in his house was the study where he kept his shelves and shelves of books.

Wambui was different from the rest of them. Somehow, she was more solid than they were. Her future was already decided. She would spend her life in Kishagi, marry Irungu, have children to keep her in her old age. Already, at the age of sixteen, she had it mapped out before her. The greatest ambition she had in the world was for a stone house like this one and like Shiku's father's house beside it.

Where had it gone so wrong for them all? Shiku found tears burning her eyes for her friend Wambui, carrier of a disease that had already claimed her child's life and threatened to destroy her life, and that of her husband, Irungu. If this decimation continued much longer, this place would become a village of children and old people with nobody in between. Shiku was glad she had got out in time. She was glad of the advantage that her education gave her in understanding and protecting herself from AIDS. And Father Ciarán had been vociferous in his fight to educate people against the epidemic. He was brave. Outspoken. Generous. And Shiku had loved him.

She lay on her back and cried, so that her tears went into her ears and tickled them. And her nose blocked up so that she had to blow it. Her sobs were so loud that she was afraid her mother would hear them from the next room. "I loved him," she whispered, "I loved him and now he is gone."

When the weeping subsided, she picked up the papers that she had taken from his house. "What did he say?" she wondered. "What did he think of what happened between us?"

She searched through his diaries, looking for a date. Yes. It was the Christmas before she went away to boarding school. Nineteen eighty-six, it was, when she was sixteen. She skipped her way through the pages. They were written in terse language. There was nothing emotional there.

Just brief, factual summaries of events, sprinkled with DVs and DGs. *Deo Volente* and *Deo Gratias.*

None of the entries for that Christmas mentioned her name. And then she found it. On 5/1/87, he had written: "Wanjiku left for school today. She is a bright student and will do well, DV."

And suddenly, she understood, without doubt, what that entry in the diary meant. It was he who had sent her away to school. She had never understood how or why her hopes and wishes had been suddenly fulfilled. Her father had been vague. Something about a bursary. But now she knew where the opportunity had come from. And she would never be able to thank him.

But why, she pondered, why had he sent her away? Was it meant as a punishment for what she did or tried to do?

She had been alone in his house that night. Irungu and Wambui had slipped off to be together. She moved from the bright fluorescent light of the kitchen into the gentler, softer space of Ciarán's study. There were books on the Scriptures and theology, his breviary, books of prayer, books on wisdom. But there was one section of the wall where there were novels in English. She picked one and sat on the small leather sofa. The book was *Lady Chatterley's Lover.* The leather creaked beneath her, but grew warm and malleable. Sitting there, absorbed in the book, she didn't notice the hours passing. And, as she read, physical sensations flooded through her young body. Desires she had not known she had were awakening. This was not the kind of love that Wambui spoke of having with Irungu. It seemed to her a dangerous kind of love, so passionate and strong.

Ciarán came in. Shiku heard him moving around the kitchen, boiling a kettle, clinking a cup, opening the fridge door. He did not know she was there. She had an idea that, if she stayed there very quietly and waited until he went to bed, she could slip out of the house. But he sauntered into the room, whistling.

"Ah, Shiku, you're still here. What are you reading?"

Mortified, she said: "Nothing."

"How d'you mean, nothing? Show me."

Desperately, she tried to hide the book behind her back.

He came over to the couch and, playfully, started wrestling with her for the book.

She was bothered by the nearness of him, flushed and embarrassed at being caught reading an unsuitable book, and still feeling that strange rising of the blood inside her. As if all the sexual parts of herself had suddenly discovered themselves and were pounding together all at once.

He caught her two wrists together and knelt on the couch almost in her lap—one knee either side of her as he put his hand behind her and grabbed the book. She remembered laughing hysterically. He was laughing, too.

"Got it! And what has the little lady been reading now?"

He lay back on the couch beside her, making a big show of examining the book. "Hardly suitable reading for an innocent young girl." His tone was becoming too serious.

"Or for a priest." She looked back at him defiantly, trying desperately to cover her humiliation, her discomfort, especially with him so close beside her.

"Shiku, ah, my little Shiku," he sighed. "The longings of the flesh are starting in you, too. The curse of the flesh . . ."

"I don't believe it's a curse. Irungu says . . ."

"Yes?" What does Irungu say?"

She was holding back her tongue, sorry to have started what she had started—Irungu's usual tirade about eunuchs refusing to be men and expecting tribesmen to follow their example. If they were serious about their Church, why wouldn't they reproduce and make themselves more little Christians, instead of stealing the young men of the tribe?

"You have longings, Father Ciarán? You are a man, after all."

She was genuinely glad, somewhere inside herself, that Irungu was wrong about him being a eunuch.

"If you only knew . . ."

She reached across to him, puckering her lips in the way she imagined a white woman would, and thrust her breasts forward against his chest, reaching up to fondle his straight, dark hair.

He pulled back, a look of shock on his face.

She had not expected that reaction. Had not known what reaction to expect, really.

Then his face scrunched up, as if he were in intense pain. His eyes clouded and filled with tears.

His lips brushed her cheek as he got to his feet. "Shiku—ah, Love, don't put me through this."

He went out. Shiku put her hand, instinctively, to her cheek. He had called her "Love." And Irungu was wrong about another thing—he had said white men couldn't cry.

7

It is from the center I begin, from these first days. I am crushed. Destroyed. All I know for definite is that I died and found absolute peace. But then I was cast out into this place of pain and doubt. At times I wonder if this is the afterlife—Purgatory or Hell? But at other times, I suspect I am alive. Dying, probably. I hope so. At least then I might be able to go back to that place where I have been.

But all these thoughts exhaust me. I lie, supine, and let my eyes trace the fine cracks in the ceiling above me. They have become familiar to me during wakeful periods which punctuate great blanks of sleep. There is brightness and darkness. I am terrified of the dark. There are no windows that I can see, just a door, always closed. Walls blank but for a single brown crucifix. Faces and figures drift through this room or through my mind. I have to concentrate to make them out. There is an Indian in a red turban. A nun in a white habit and apron. Sometimes I see Shiku, looking sad and troubled. The face of Father Madden appears, also. These images are slightly out of focus and not quite real.

I become aware of movement, of bustle, of voices, of more faces than usual looking in at me. But I sleep and, when I wake, the room is changed. A dim light bulb, swathed in yellow cotton, hangs from the center of the ceiling. This mustn't be Hell then, I tell myself. Hell would never allow such comforts as the soft glow of that bulb during the long hours of night.

There is a gecko living in the corner. He makes quick forays out across the ceiling to pounce on his prey; the small flies and mosquitoes have no chance against his swift, lethal attacks. I envy the gecko his mobility and the way he is so solidly there, within his skin and yet almost transparent, appearing not to be there. I wish that I could blend like that, change the color of my skin, and not always be so obvious—a white man in Africa.

Africa. Am I still here, then? I sniff the air. There is a smell of rotting cabbage. It tells me nothing. The air is warm—tropical, maybe. I manage to raise my right hand to where I can see it. My fingers are still covered in pinkish European skin.

There is a woman whom I do not know. She has a round, black, smiling face. I watch, as if from a great distance, as she tends to my body. She moves in a busy, bustling way. Her hands are gentle. Always, after she leaves, I feel a surge of euphoria, cessation of pain and, then, I sleep.

Sometimes, I see the face of Shiku looking down at

me. I haven't the strength to say her name or to ask if she is real or where I am. Then, one day, unasked, she tells me. I feel the touch of her fingers on my brow. "It is okay," she says. "You are with me in Peponi."

Her words confuse me. *Peponi* is the Swahili word for Heaven. But I have been to Heaven and I know that it is nothing like this.

Something of my agitation communicates itself to her. "Peponi Road," she clarifies. "You will be safer here."

Memory returns then, briefly, filling in the missing details. Yes, Shiku lives with her husband in a house on Peponi Road. This is where they must have brought me.

But there are other memories struggling to assert themselves. They bring with them the whiff of terror. I will not allow them into my conscious mind. For now, it is enough that I am here with Shiku and I want to believe her, that I am safe.

The face of Father Madden still appears, sometimes, but I doubt that it is real. Surely, this is an image I have brought with me from childhood. He is completely out of context here, in this place. So when I see him again, I scrutinize the features. It is an older face than I re-member, collapsed somehow, and the eyes have reddened and gone slack. The hair is snowy white. I remember it as brown. His words, when I listen to them, are not any that I have heard him speak before. "I will take you home," he says. "Home to Ireland."

"No." The vehemence of that word takes such effort

that it wears me out. I watch his face still mouthing, but his words no longer register.

His presence here at this time puzzles me. If it is a memory from childhood, then why remember it now? And why remember it differently to the way it was? Or if it is a dream, why dream about him now, after all these years? And why does he make me feel uneasy? Why would he want to take me back to Ireland? How can I go back there?

I realize that I have strung a whole series of thoughts together and that must mean that my mind, at least, is mending. The smiling lady notices that I am more alert.

"Ah, bwana," she says, delightedly. "Today you can know me. My name is Esther." She punches up the pillows from under my head and props me against them in a sitting position. I wince as she moves me. "There, now. Comfortable?"

I nod, although I am uncomfortable. From here I can see more of my surroundings. Nurse Esther fiddles with a needle strapped to the back of my left hand. There is a mirror opposite me and I watch her reflection as she fits a new bag of fluid to the pole behind my bed. Of course! How else could I have stayed here so long without eating? I am pleased with this discovery. It proves that there is some sense and logic in what is happening to me now.

Still, I have this vacant feeling as she works on me: washing, massaging, dressing my wounds, coming and going with bedpans. My mind has no wish to engage itself with bodily functions, with what works and what doesn't; it flinches away from thinking about the extent of those injuries. I absent myself and am glad that my body has a caretaker during my absence. My ability to withdraw like this reminds me that I am still between living and dying.

I watch the mirror. It shows a window behind me. Outside there is sunshine and jacaranda trees in leaf. The curtains are yellow cotton, patterned with tiny black giraffes. They match the light shade. I run my finger over little black giraffes on the yellow bedspread. There are wrought iron bars on the window.

It is night and I am wakened by a scream. I pull the thin blanket up over my head and shrink down into the deepest part of myself. Fear centers me, so that my thinking self is buffered within my body. The extremities of hands and feet feel far away and terribly exposed. I lie, shivering. My heart is thundering as if it will burst. It is not death I fear, but pain, wounding, the casual infliction of violence. The realization that everything that I am can be crushed out of existence as carelessly as a cockroach can be trodden underfoot.

I hear the scream again. Thin. High-pitched. It is not a human sound but the cry of a frightened animal. It comes from close by, almost as if it were in the room with me. A scratching sound comes from behind me, from outside the window. Again, I smell rotting cabbages, sour and vaguely familiar. Like the smell from the hutches in Kishagi. Rabbits. Even here, in the city, they must keep them for food. The scrabbling sounds continue and I am happy that this animal, whatever he is, has survived whatever danger threatened him. I have known the shape and depth of his fear. That gives me an affinity with him. He is probably safe enough, I tell myself. If he is a rabbit, he is, most likely, kept in some kind of enclosure to protect him from predators. And he can burrow down into the earth. There are bars on the windows here. There are grilles and padlocks on the doors, I'm sure. And nobody knows I am here. I am probably safe, too.

When Nurse Esther comes today, she insists on propping me on my left side. "You will get bedsores, bwana," she scolds. "Your circulation will stop, *kabisa*." I am not used to being called bwana. It strikes me that even the nurse has not been told many details of who I am or what has happened to me.

Waking out of a deep sleep, I find that I am still lying on my left side, facing the door. A child is staring at me. One thumb is stuck, shyly, into her mouth and her big brown eyes are wide with curiosity. When she sees my eyelids open, she jumps and shrinks back, preparing to flee. I don't want her to go.

"Hello."

She doesn't answer but lingers, hesitant, the thumb still in her mouth. She has obviously been warned against disturbing me.

I make another effort: "What is your name?" My voice comes out coarse and soft like broken eggshells.

She hugs herself, swaying, so that her skirt furls and unfurls around her thin legs. "Muthoni," she whispers and giggles.

"Muthoni. My name is Ciarán."

"Keerawn." She pronounces it exactly as I say it.

Déjà vu. I am outside myself again, remembering. Kishagi. Another time. A teenage girl. This same conversation, almost.

"Wanjiku," she said, "but I am always called Shiku."

"And which name do you prefer?"

"Shiku."

"Shiku, my name is Ciarán."

"Keerawn," she repeated precisely. And laughed. "Do you know what they call you? *Kilani.*"

"Where I come from Killarney is the name of a town."

"Killarney," she repeated, putting all the R's and L's in their correct places. "You see," she explained, "in Kikuyu language, R's and L's are the same." She rolled the sound on her tongue, somewhere midway between an L and an R.

"We have that exact sound in Irish, as well," I said.

Shiku's daughter has inherited her mother's facility for language.

"Muthoni? Do you keep rabbits in the garden?"

I have touched on a subject that makes her shyness evaporate.

"Sungura is my rabbit. I call him that name because he is clever, like the *sungura* in the stories."

"He is not for eating, then."

She looks at me, indignantly. "Nobody can eat this Sungura. He is my friend."

"Sungura is lucky to have you as a friend."

"Will I bring you to see him?"

"Maybe. If I am better."

I have been turned on my right side and cannot see the door as a visitor is ushered into the room. He draws a chair up beside me and sits. It is Father Madden.

"Father. I thought I'd dreamed you up."

He lets out a short laugh and gives me a pitying look. "How are you feeling, Keerin?"

"Alive. And it's Ciarán, like the saint."

This is crazy. Past and present keep rolling into one. I had this conversation with him when I was seven years old.

"Ah," this older Father Madden says: "But the saint was Keerin, wasn't he? From the Latin. The Irish version would have been later."

I look at black hairs poking out of his nostrils and I feel like a small boy again. "I don't know, Father."

"I am to arrange for your return to Ireland. It isn't safe for you to stay here after what has happened."

"I am perfectly safe."

"You should never trust the woolly-head. That's what got you into this bother."

This is the man who influenced me and set me on the path I have taken. It was in his footsteps that I came here, to Africa. If this is what he believes, then everything I have done, or tried to do, has been compromised by association.

"Father Madden, you're insulting my friends."

"You can't ever call them friend. That's the mistake you made."

Shiku's voice butts into the conversation. "Ciarán is tired. I must ask you to leave." It is said with a deadly coldness.

The priest gets up to leave. He seems oblivious of any wrongdoing. His words float back: "The doctor will inform me when you are well enough to be moved."

"Gobshite!" I murmur and feel that I could cry with shame.

I am still here, lying on my right side, when a big jackrabbit hops across the floor and stops on his hunkers, front paws in the air. His long ears and nose are twitching and he blinks at me with pink, albino eyes.

I am inclined to disbelieve what I see. But, then, this is a place where everything has been made strange. Today, I have even questioned the truth of my own name. There can't be much more to lose, so I take a risk.

"*Habari, Bwana Sungura?*" I say aloud. (How are you, Mr. Rabbit?)

"*Mzuri,*" (Fine) comes a small voice. "*Habari yaku, Baba Keerawn?*"

Baba—Father. I'm not sure whether the title fits me anymore. I test a new one, *Bwana*—Mister. "*Bwana* Ciarán," I say. "*Bwana* Ciarán *ni mzuri.*"

The air erupts with laughter and Muthoni peeps at me around the end of the bed. "Ah, you are clever like Sungura! How did you know that this rabbit speaks only *Kiswahili?*" She scoops the rabbit up in her arms and sits on the floor, cuddling him; her black plaits tumble over his white fur.

"I heard Sungura talking outside my window."

Muthoni looks up at me with shining eyes. "Really?"

"Really."

"Sungura likes you, *Bwana* Keerawn."

The doctor wears a red turban over neat whiskers and a bright smile. He tweezes stitches out of my flesh, explaining that the internal stitching was done with special thread and will dissolve. I marvel at him. That in an emergency such as mine he had the presence of mind to think what threads to use, with death already snatching me from under his furiously stitching fingers.

I look at the whorls of cloth in the doctor's turban as he bends his head over me, listening to my heart. As he prods and pokes, I see his kind face, his sallow skin, his clean, manicured fingernails.

"Doctor?"

"Mmm?"

"I died."

He takes a step back and looks at me intensely. Then he considers for a long time before he speaks. His chin begins the nod before his words find themselves. "Yes," he says. "Technically, you did."

"Did you bring me back?"

Again, the nod. The slow formation of words. "A man such as you has much good to do in this life. I weighed that against the danger."

"Danger?"

He nods again. "Brain damage." Then smiles. "Obviously there is none." His grin is broad and triumphant.

"How long was I . . . gone?"

"Twenty minutes."

"Am I going to live?"

He pauses. Smiles. Considers. "That is in the hands of your god. Having brought you so far, perhaps he will not abandon you now."

"He's already abandoned me. It was you who saved my life." I feel betrayed and angry. Angry with a god who failed to show himself and with this man who presumed to play god with me.

But the doctor is a devout man and does not share my view of what has happened. He makes light of it. "If you were Hindu, we might say you were reincarnated, but we cannot expect this with Christians."

How can I tell him that I didn't want to be brought back from where I was? It would be wrong to seem ungrateful to him. "What is your medical opinion, Doctor?"

"Ah." We are back in his familiar realm and he is, immediately, more at ease. With his finger, he traces the line of my wounds in the air above my chest and stomach. "You see, these cuts were inflicted with a *panga*—which is essentially a digging tool. And, fortunately, the blade of this *panga* was blunt, so, instead of slicing, you could say it dug through you, skipping and bruising and bursting the flesh. Where it went deep enough, it damaged the internal organs. I suspect that these injuries are like rips or puncture wounds. There may be more serious damage, or infection, but you are still too weak for further investigation or surgery."

"What caused me to . . . die?"

"Your heart stopped. Injury, shock, loss of blood, any or all of these things; I do not know. But it has been stable since and I am . . ." he pauses, stroking his beard, "cautiously optimistic."

He looks pleased with himself. My presence here, however frail, authenticates him. I can see happiness in his eyes as he beholds me. Pleasure in the movement of his lips. There is no greater good a man can do than to save the life of another. This is the philosophy that keeps him, day after day, peering down throats and probing the bleeding depths of people. This is what makes him a good man. Unlike that other . . . the one with the *panga* in his hand. But I won't think of him. Not now.

After the doctor has left, I notice a batik that hangs on the wall beside the door. It is an abstract—unusual

among African art of this type. The background is brown
and beige and there are bold shapes outlined in black. I
push my mind to grapple with the images contained in
them. Sometimes I think I can make out a pot, but then
the image recedes so that I am no longer sure if it is
there, or if I have seen it. And underneath, I can make
little sense of what I see. Some golden objects and a
russet-colored area at the center. And outside—wings.
Are they wings? The images swim in and out of focus. I
see the pot. Definitely an African pot, terra-cotta-col-
ored and patterned with black and cream.

"You are looking much better."

"Shiku! Come in."

She sits tentatively at the edge of my bed. "Maybe
you are not ready for visitors."

"You're hardly a visitor."

She smiles. Her lips quiver back from her white teeth.
In profile, she is like a perfect ebony carving: her cheek-
bones high and fine and her hair, in narrow plaits, drawn
up to the top of her head. Her beauty shocks me.

She senses my eyes on her.

"Shiku, tell me about that batik. What is it?"

"Oh, I am so sorry," she says, leaping to her feet.
"Does it offend you?" Already, she has her hand on the
frame and is lifting it from its nail.

"Please don't move it. I just wondered what it was
about, that's all."

"You are joking me?"

"I thought I saw a pot."

"It is a pot they carry between them. They are lovers."

There is a hint of mischief in Shiku's eye as she replaces the batik and turns to look at me. "You seriously mean you cannot see this?"

"A pot, maybe. That's all."

She runs her hands over the cloth. "See here, this is her head. This is his head. They are together, kissing. And below these—the funnel, on his side, is a phallic symbol and on her side . . ." she pauses for an instant, to judge my reaction, then shrugs and continues in a rush of words, "a calabash with an opening at the center—a receptacle waiting to be filled. And behind these, the hearts together, and a communal belly or womb—the inner parts of themselves, joined. But up here, above all this, is the pot they carry between them—the symbol of their togetherness. You would call it love, I suppose."

I look sadly at the picture, seeing nothing but abstract shapes. "Maybe it is visible only to the initiated."

"Nobody has had a problem interpreting it. But then, as you say, they are not celibate. I am sorry."

Her "sorry" covers more than just my inability to understand the picture. Celibacy is a state that is incomprehensible to her. In her eyes it makes me less than a man.

"Ciarán." Shiku's voice is hesitant. "There is something I must tell you. I hope you will not be angry."

"What could you do, ever, to make me angry?"

"I was there, in Kishagi, on the night you were attacked.

I believed you were dead. My father had taken you away in the car. I couldn't know if these murderers were still there, hiding, or if they would burn your house. Or if other people would come. Your papers were scattered on your desk. I wasn't sure if they could be used against you if they fell into the wrong hands. So, I took them."

"My papers?"

"Diaries. Letters."

"Did you read them?"

"Yes. I did not know what I should do, if I should destroy them or if I should send them to Ireland, to your mother."

"You didn't destroy them, did you?"

"No. They are here."

"Thank God."

"Ciarán, I know it was you who sent me away to school."

"Did I say that, in my diary?"

"Not directly. But I understood it. How can I thank you enough?"

"Oh, Shiku, you don't need to."

"It is because of you that I have everything—Julius, Muthoni, this place, my teaching job. Without you, I would not even be myself, as I am now."

"You did those things for yourself. I only wrote a few letters."

Julius appears and I lie looking up at his broad, hand-some face. He wears traditional dress, a knee-length brown and purple smock, embroidered at the neck and worn over baggy trousers of the same material. This is the first time I have seen him since I have been here. He is always silent in my company and I am never sure if his silence signifies respect or indifference. Now, lounging in the doorway and looking down at me from his immense height, he exudes strength and masculinity. As he moves, a ring glints on his left hand. It is the ring I blessed on the day that Shiku placed it on his finger. Already, she was visibly pregnant with his child. I remember thinking that he wasn't a good enough man for her.

He steps forward, suddenly, and takes my right hand in his, lifting his thumb and engaging mine in the customary clasp of friendship.

"You are welcome in my house for as long as you need to stay."

Julius smiles and is gone before I can even thank him.

I drift into a dreamless sleep and when I awake it is night-time, but not entirely dark. There is a crack of brightness under the door. The curtains are still open and the mirror reflects light from the garden. Outside, there is the sound of laughter and bustle. People chatter excitedly. Suddenly, the night erupts with a loud swell of voices and a series of explosions, sharp and crackling. The mirror shows colors cascading down the sky: bursts of pink, red, green, purple, and shimmering white.

Shiku appears, silhouetted in the shining space of

the doorway. She wears a headdress and a flowing robe.

"Ciarán, are you awake?" A half-whisper.

"Yes."

She rushes to me and hugs my shoulders, carefully avoiding my sore parts; she kisses me on one cheek, again on the other, then on the first again. "Happy Millennium!"

"What happened to Christmas?"

"You were in hospital. You missed it."

Shiku hugs me again, kisses me three times again. "You almost missed the Millennium, too."

"I almost missed everything."

"Will I leave the curtains open so that you can see the fireworks?" Her voice is breathless and there is a high color in her cheeks. She is slightly tipsy, I suspect.

"You can close them. And put the light on, please."

"Oh, I nearly forgot!" Her high heels and long skirt exaggerate the wag of her buttocks as she saunters from the room. The smell of roasting goat meat wafts through from the garden. A tape recorder has been turned on full volume and the fast, high-pitched jingling of music drowns out the clamor of voices.

When Shiku returns, she plops a bundle of diaries and papers on the pillow beside me. "Does the noise bother you?"

"Don't worry. I'll sleep if I need to."

"I wish you could join us."

"It's okay. Really."

She pauses in the doorway, as if to say something. Thinks better of it. Moves suddenly. Catches her heel in the hem of her dress. Stumbles. Rights herself. Giggles.

Outside, the music has slowed: "*Malaika, na kupenda, Malaika*"—I love you, angel. The door clicks closed behind her.

What has she been reading in my diaries, I wonder? How much does she know? I pick out a notebook and riffle through the pages, searching for a date. January, 1987, was it? Yes. 5/1/87. "*Wanjiku left for school today. She is a bright student and will do well, DV.*" Is that all I said? Good God! Is there nothing here of that immense struggle? A bright student. Sweet Jesus!

I search the surrounding pages, looking for other references, and go through the other diaries to find significant dates in my life. Everything is recorded in the same terse phrases sprinkled with pious exclamations. Why did I even bother to keep a diary?

10/8/96—"Father died today. RIP."

2/2/99—"Baby Waithera Irungu died of AIDS. RIP."

11/18/99—"Kishagi market burnt down."

11/19/99—"Christian burial for 'arsonists' despite opposition."

I read with a sense of panic. If this is the only testament to my life, then I am leaving nothing behind.

One of the notebooks has some pages left. There is a pen still stuck in the spine. I have a night that I thought was lost to me. I have a pen and a blank page. What I write tonight, however inadequate, will be some real thing left of me when I am gone. I write the date. *1/1/00.* It seems insubstantial. Too small. Too empty. Something about that 00. I cross it out and begin again: *1/1/2000.* That seems too self-important. I prefer 00. Nowhere. It says more about where I am.

8

Nurse Esther unhooks me from my drip. She bullies and half carries me up three steps to the bathroom. There, she strips me and lifts me, as gently as she can, into the tepid bath water, laced with salt. I'm surprised by her strength and by the ease with which she handles me. But when I see myself naked, I realize that I have shrunk. My body has been reduced to skin and bone. I am barely here.

The sticky tape adheres to hairs on my chest and stomach. I brace myself for the wrench as she rips off the dressings one by one. "I am so sorry," she says, "but quickest is best."

I am unused to being exposed like this with a woman. But she is busy and efficient, concentrating on my wounds. "Oh my, oh my," she croons as she works, scooping salty water with the pink palms of her hands.

"Ah, bwana, I do not know how you are still living after this. It must be too hard to kill an Irish."

"Do you think I'll survive?"

"Only Ngai can know these things."

Ngai, creator and divider of the universe—Esther's universe. Perhaps an African god would prove more reliable than my own—the god of the Irish—the god of the one, true, holy, Catholic and apostolic Church. I have never felt like this before. I have never, even for a moment, doubted.

Nurse Esther hitches her hand beneath my knees and pulls me down so that I am lying in the bath. She leans over me and I feel the warmth of her breath on me as she splashes and channels water over my wounds.

I consider Esther's unshakeable belief in her Ngai. What would she think, I wonder, if I told her where I have been? When Africans die, their spirits go back to the earth, not up to a higher place, as ours do. Was I up? It didn't feel like up. I didn't soar above the bed and watch the red whorls of the doctor's turban as he carefully chose his threads. I experienced none of that. It felt more like falling.

The salty water flows in rivulets along the ridges of my wounds. For the first time, I look at my mutilated flesh. It is livid red and far too sore to touch. I have an image of my father gutting fish—the neat slicing open of the belly from gills to anus. I can see what the doctor described: the ridges, the puckers, the skips, the bruises: the work of a heavy, blunt blade. For an instant I see the *panga* raised, falling. For a millisecond, I see the

eyes of my attacker. They are smoldering. Obsessed. Killer
eyes. My stomach lurches. I feel the pain. I gasp.

Esther notices. "Salt water is good for healing, yes?"
Strange, but I thought the eyes of my assassin should
be cold. Empty.

My eyes travel down along the lines of the wounds.
Will I ever be able to reclaim that flesh? I ask myself.
Will I ever be able to touch those scars with my own
fingers and not flinch away from the contact?

I let my eyes follow down and down to where the
scars get lost among the pubic hairs. My phallus is bob-
bing, pale and inert, in the water. A virgin. Untouched.
Uninjured in this attack. I think of the lifelong battle I
have waged against it. How I have scourged myself with
guilt and blame every time it budged out of its restful
state. How I have curbed it, denied it, disallowed it,
threatened it, and fought against it. But how it never
obeyed me, never lay calmly, snugly, submissively, especially in the presence of a woman. Until now.

Esther pulls the plug, stands me up, and wipes me
dry, checking as she does for pressure sores.

"It is time for you to move out of this bed. To sit
for a while in the chair. To walk slowly, slowly. Keep
your blood going."

She has been saying this for several days now, and I
have not heeded her.

"You will get blood clots. Bedsores," she scolds, click-
ing her tongue at me.

Off the corner of my room, beside the bathroom door, I have noticed a little blind end of a corridor. Into this tiny niche a dressing table has been built, with cupboards above and a little vanity unit with a mirror. On this, the thirtieth day of my reprieve, I take my notebook and climb the three steps. At each tread, I pause and gasp for breath, my heart straining with the effort. I force each foot forward and upward. Gaining ground. At the top, I collapse into the chair before the mirror. There are three mirrors actually, the smaller outside pair hinged to the central panel.

I catch sight of a reflection. It is the image of my father as he was when I last saw him—hair standing on end, cheeks hollowed, eyes sunken and troubled, the skeletal grin of death already stretching the skin of the face. Why am I imagining him? I peer more closely at the thin, aged face and recognize a tiny blue circle below the right ear—a pockmark from a childhood illness. My mark. Is that old man really me? I smile and my death's head leers at me. "Your time will not be long," he says.

"I have today," I answer and slam the mirrors shut on him.

I look with dull eyes at the hemmed-in space of my self-chosen cell. I feel an affinity with the monks of old as they lifted their quills to copy down the gospels of the new religion. But I will copy nothing. I will hammer away at truth. I will strain the limits of language to create a new version of this estranged world, so that I can live in it, for whatever time is left. A new version of myself that will fill the emptiness left by my going.

My mother's Nivea Creme was in a flat, blue box on her dressing table. She had a hairbrush with colored cloth on the back. When she let her hair down from the tight bun in which she usually wore it, it reached right down to her waist. She would sit on the stool, brushing it out, sparks flying from the brush. Glints in her hair matched the flecks in her green eyes. The dressing table mirror was really three mirrors with the two smaller ones hinged to the full-length one in the center. I loved closing the side mirrors in and out, getting different reflections of her, of myself, of her hairbrush, her Nivea Creme, her lovely auburn hair.

I could skew images, reflecting my mother's blue Nivea box and catching that reflection again in the opposite mirror. I could make each reflection reflect, not only the original but itself, so that there were blue boxes going away into the distance, getting smaller and smaller.

There was a ridge at the edge of the glass. A bevel, my mother called it. Bev-el. If I caught an image in it I could make the image warp.

In the center mirror my mother was smiling. Her tummy was fat and her hand was flat against it. She had a funny, dreamy look in her eyes. I caught her smile in the bevel at the edge of the side mirror and moved it so that her smile twisted. The closer I pulled the edges together the more her face distorted.

"See, Mammy, see, I can make you cry!" I was excited

by my own power as I clicked and clacked, creating more and more bizarre images.

When I looked back into the central mirror there were tears reflected there. My mother's hands were clutching her stomach and her face was puckering in pain.

"I'm sorry, Mammy, I'm sorry—I'll put the mirrors back."

The only picture I knew of baby Declan was a picture in stone. He was a roundy-faced cherub with little angel wings. My mother brought me with her nearly every day. We picked bunches of flowers by the roadside—daisies or wild woodbines—and put them in a jam jar beside his picture. Then I would have to be very quiet while she talked to him.

One day, after she had been kneeling for a long time, her lips moving, but no words coming out, I asked her: "Can Baby Declan hear you?"

"Yes, of course."

"Where is he?"

"God took him to Heaven."

"Where's Heaven?"

"Up there." She gestured vaguely toward the sky.

"Can he see us?"

"He's looking down on us right now. Our own little angel."

She had gone dreamy again, tears standing in her eyes. A wisp of hair that had worked free from the bun was falling across her face and she dabbed at it, irritably, with the back of her hand as she rearranged the flowers for the umpteenth time, and scattered and moved little white pebbles on the ground around the jar.

"Mammy, why did God take Baby Declan up to Heaven?"

"Because he was good."

She blessed herself and took me by the hand. Our feet scrunched the gravel path to the gates of the grave-yard. As we walked back down the country road, past the green pond, we never spoke. It was no use asking more questions. She either wouldn't listen or wouldn't answer.

Our front door was huge and green. It had a knocker that was a black fist holding a laurel wreath. The knocker was high up and hard to reach. There was a bell with a white center that said PRESS (it was one of the first words I learned to read). Mostly, I remember the door lying open and the bright green summer light filtering through the leaves of the trees. There were six steps down to the gravel drive that ran beside the house to the tumbledown sheds at the back of the garden. The stables, my mother called them, and talked of better times, old times, when I imagined horses galloping and carriages rolling past our door.

I used to run my Dinky cars up and down those steps, in and out between the railings. I would park them beside the iron shoe-scraper and catch their wheels in the grooves between the stones. Talking aloud. Always weaving stories in my head.

There were winter nights when the door was closed and creaky shutters barred the windows as gales shrieked and rain dripped through the porch roof into a bucket in the hall. On those nights I would lie spread-eagled on the hearth rug, reading. My father would poke the fire and adjust the throat—that is what the thing was called that opened and closed the chimney when the flames got too high. The dog and cat would curl up beside me as the wind moaned in the chimney. Gargoyles stared down at us from the over-mantel.

My mother had lived all her life in that house, surrounded by what she called her "relics of old decency." I didn't know what that meant. It had something to do with those being good times and these being bad.

In the years before my sister was born, I seemed to spend all my time with my mother. We visited the cathedral almost as often as the graveyard. There were early morning Masses, devotions, retreats, benedictions, and Stations of the Cross. The cathedral was a vast gallery of altars, shrines, mosaics, carvings, pictures, and stained-glass windows. I would catch the light through the stained glass and see the Biblical stories and the lives of saints flash into life. And high up above the spires and statues and the carved angels, I would see a little cherub looking down. You didn't have to speak aloud so he could hear you, therefore he must be able to read thoughts. Whenever I thought of my mind lying open like that, something sinful would come into my head, like a bad word I didn't want to think about. And I would have to try very hard not to think about that thing because he was listening and he was good—much better than I could ever be.

My hand shakes slightly as I pull back the side mirrors and look straight at my reflection. I appraise myself. My withered face, my eyes dark with visions few have seen this side of the grave. I died, I tell myself. I died and there was just peace, absolute peace, unlike any I have known. Eternal peace, I would have said.

But wasn't that Heaven? A place or state of perfect happiness, according to the Catholic definition. It was that. But I was cheated out of it. And retrospectively, I feel cheated by it. Because there was no face of God. There were no angels. There were no trumpets. Not that I'm a person who likes fuss. But should there not have been some recognition for my life? For my work? For the spiritual life? For the years of fighting against my physical wants?

Is that it? Did I want to be patted on the back and told: "Well done, you have lived an exemplary life. You have done the right thing"?

Yes. I needed to be told I had done the right thing. That's the nub. Heaven was okay. I can find no fault with Heaven, really. It was before that that the problem started. With my death. Before I gave up the struggle and let go. It was in that moment when you see things clearly. You know you're dying. It's finished. It was then that the conviction came to me: "My life has been a waste. I have tried to be divine and failed to be human."

And nothing that followed then or since has altered that conviction.

Why was I spared? Why was I not allowed to die when I had died? In the last moments, I fought to live, before I knew what dying was. And now I know and I would rather be dead.

The doctor tells me he is cautiously optimistic that I will live. There is a part of me that rejects his optimism. A part of me that would rather die. There is a part of me that fears that the doctor may be right and that I may live. That part of me is afraid of the process. Afraid of having to go back through all that dying to get there. Then again, I am alive. My feeble body still clings on here. But life is something so easily taken.

I never thought I could die. I always thought of myself as indestructible, somehow. As if the universe worked itself around me—me, the thinking, conscious "I" at the center. We all know about death, yes, in an abstract sort of way. But it is something that happens to somebody else. Not to me. And not at the age of forty-two.

The part of me that believed in a future has been seriously disillusioned. The future has shut down on me.

Here I am, before this mirror in Peponi. And not only am I physically destroyed, but spiritually bereft. My entire model of the universe and the place of man within it has been shattered by my experience. I no longer know who or what I am or what is the scheme of things.

Life that used to be so precious is suddenly empty, mean-
ingless, threatening.

It was easy being part of a belief system. You didn't
have to *know* anything, prove anything. All you had to
do was believe. And I did. Not only did I believe, I
dedicated my life to bringing that belief to others. But
when I died it ceased to be a belief. It became a reality
that didn't match the belief. So, now, what do I believe?
That I am alive. Yes, I believe I am alive. I believe that I
am in Shiku's house in Peponi Road. I have no proof of
any of this, actually. It is becoming a new belief system.
I believe in this little girl, Muthoni. She seems more
real than anything. I believe I found myself talking to a
rabbit. I found that I no longer believe for definite in
my own name. I believe that Father Madden is not the
man I believed him to be. Not that he is an imposter
now, but that he was then, when he told me about the
children in Africa. When he fired me with enthusiasm
for this missionary life. I don't believe I am a priest any
more. Because my priestly vocation was about bringing
people to God and I no longer believe that He exists.

Shiku is surprised to see me out of bed and sitting
by the mirror.

"Ciarán. You're getting better!" Her tone belies the
enthusiasm of her words. She looks awful. Her face is
all swollen and the whites of her eyes are blood-red.

"Shiku, what's wrong?"

"Julius has gone." She can't hold her tears. "He has

gone to America," she sobs. "He is finishing his doctorate." Shiku scrubs at her face with a handkerchief.

"For how long?"

"Three or four months. It is not so bad." A flood of tears overcomes her best efforts at composure. "I just hate it when he goes. Excuse me, Ciarán."

Muthoni scuttles in with a book under her arm. "Will you read me a story, bwana Ciarán?"

"Of course, Muthoni. Which story?"

We settle ourselves and her book up on the bed. "This one about the *sungura*. It is my favorite."

We find the page and I begin to read: "In olden times, there was a rabbit, a hippopotamus, and an elephant. They lived in the middle of a very small island that had many hills. The hippopotamus and the elephant treated the rabbit like a slave. They forced the *sungura* to serve them because he was so small.

"As he slaved and slaved for his masters, he was thinking of many ways to escape. But he was afraid that he could not swim all the way from that island. So, he thought of a plan to pay the elephant and the hippo back, to teach them some manners.

"One morning he got up and found a hoe, a *panga,* and a crowbar. Carrying these on his hip, he went to a hill that was just halfway between their house and the water. Well, he started to dig a tunnel right through that hill from one side to the other. It took seven days to dig the tunnel and he was really tired when he was finished.

"The rabbit set out, happily, to look for the elephant. He found him, standing near the house, chewing the cud. From a distance he called to him. 'Are you well, master elephant?'

"The elephant kept chewing. 'Well, boy. Why are you bothering me like this when I am resting? Is this how you repay me after all I've done for you?'

"'No, master elephant,' said the rabbit, 'I didn't come here to disturb you. I came here to bring you a present of a cow that gives plenty of the best milk.'

"This elephant swallowed and said, 'If you have really brought me a present, why are you standing there on your own? Where is this present?'

"The *sungura* showed him a big rope that he had brought with him. 'I've just bought this rope for tying the cow. If you tie this end around your leg, I will go and tie the other end to the cow over there. Then, when I shake the rope it will be a sign to you to pull that cow of yours.'

"But the elephant did not trust the *sungura*. He asked him, 'If there really is a cow, why don't you tie that rope to him and bring him here?'

"'I am very small,' replied the rabbit, 'Too small to bring you this cow. But you are strong enough to pull him, no problem.'

"The *sungura* left the elephant to tie one end of the rope around his hind leg. Then he took the other end of the rope and passed right through the tunnel and came out on the other side of the hill.

"He found the hippopotamus lying down, pretending to be a dark rock in the water. When the hippo saw the *sungura*, he ignored him and continued with his game.

"But the rabbit spoke to him politely. 'Hello, my master.'

"With his mouth full of water, the hippo answered him, 'Hello, boy. Why have you come here?'

"'I have brought you a very nice present,' replied the *sungura*. 'This rope I am holding is tied to a cow. He is asleep over there. So I want to tie this rope to your waist so that you can pull him when he wakes.'

"The hippopotamus was not sure. He said, 'You, *sungura*—if you try to trick me, I will snuff you out as I would put out a fire. I think that you are a clever trickster.'

"'No, no, master hippopotamus,' the *sungura* insisted, 'I could not deceive somebody like you. I swear I always tell the pure truth.'

"The hippo tied the rope around his waist. Then the rabbit set out and climbed to the top of the hill, so that he could watch the hippopotamus and the elephant.

"After a while the big animals tried pulling hard on the rope. They both thought they were pulling a cow, but they couldn't understand why the rope was so hard to pull. They tried. And tried again, but where was the cow?

"Well, the elephant stopped chewing his cud and the hippopotamus came out of the water and they began to pull that rope really hard. They pulled and pulled, but they were not able to pull each other.

"They were stuck there as if by magic, barely moving one tiny step and being pulled back to the same spot.

"During all of this the *sungura* was above on the hill watching them. Well, he laughed and he laughed and he laughed until his sides began to ache. He had to stop looking to stop laughing.

"When the *sungura* was tired from watching them pulling and pulling and getting nowhere, he took the *panga*. He went quietly down to the side where the hippopotamus was and went into a clump of trees. There, he reached the rope and cut it through the middle. The elephant fell over and the hippopotamus fell into the water. Then they stayed where they had fallen and they were panting.

"After cutting the rope, the rabbit went into hiding. He didn't want those animals to find him.

"A day and many more passed, and the hippopotamus was out for a walk with the elephant. They were finishing off their morning calls when the elephant asked, 'Tell me, have you seen that *sungura*? He pulled that rope and then he vanished, just like his cow.'

"'He tricked us,' said the hippopotamus, feeling very sorry. And the elephant asked: 'Why did he go away like that? I do not understand it.'

"The hippopotamus answered him: 'I think it was because we were always pulling and dragging him.'"

Muthoni squeals with enthusiasm. "Ah, that *sungura*! That *sungura*! He is so clever."

And I find myself laughing with her at *sungura* and his antics and how he always wins out.

The story of the elephant and the hippo holds me sleepless long into the night. I keep seeing my father and myself on either side of that rope. Neither of us were bad people in our way, but we would never budge an inch. We just pulled and pulled against each other.

9

From the moment the telephone rang, before I heard my sister's voice on the line, it seemed that I knew.

"Ciarán, this is Oonagh. Bad news, I'm afraid."

I thought of my mother as I had last seen her, standing, biting back tears as she waved goodbye from the doorway. I thought of my father at Cork Airport, opening the boot for me to take out my suitcase. At each parting it was in all our minds—is this the last time we will ever see each other?

There was static on the line and my sister's words were getting lost and garbled. Out of it all, I distinguished one word: "Dad." I remembered the firm grip of his handshake. The averted eyes.

"What?" There was a time lag and our voices ate into each other.

"Sudden . . . in and out of consciousness." And then, a moment of clarity: "Ciarán, he's asking to see you."

"Oh." During twelve years of exile, I had rehearsed many versions of this conversation. In most of them, it

was my mother, the delicate one, who had been taken
ill. And in all of them, I was being called back for a
funeral. But now my father was still alive and would
cling on, no doubt, until I came home. There would be
time for a final reconciliation. Or confrontation. Why
couldn't he just die without dragging me into it?

"Ciarán, are you still there?"

"But he wasn't sick, was he?"

"Cancer . . . think . . . long time . . . pretended . . ."

How typical of the old man to try to fight it through
and refuse help until it was too late. I put the telephone
down with a sense of frustration mingled with disbelief.
Then I picked up the phone again to make arrangements
for a flight home.

Nicolas, (our house man, sacristan, and general
minder of the compound) said he'd drive me to the
airport. The trip would give him an opportunity to visit
his daughter, Shiku, in Nairobi, and he would bring my
car back to Kishagi in the morning. He threw my bat-
tered brown suitcase into the back of the white Peugeot
pickup.

"Fatha John will mind the parish," Nicolas reassured
me as he ground the gear lever into a shuddery first
gear.

His words conjured up a vision of John Kariuki, the
deacon, masquerading as a priest while I was gone. I
should warn Nicolas that Kariuki wasn't authorized to
perform sacraments. But then, I thought, the sincerity

of the people was not at issue. And if they related to their God and if He heard them, then a sacrament of sorts would happen anyway. This reassured me, as we drove out of the church compound and through the sprawl of the village of Kishagi, its houses and huts secluded by banana trees. Cocks crowed and hens scattered ahead of us. Of course the Bishop would get to hear of it. Well, it would be a welcome change to have John Kariuki incurring Episcopal wrath! I chuckled and let it go.

The car slowed for speed bumps beside the Kishagi Market. Noise, bustle, and raucous music reached us across the hazy heat of the dusty road. Little stalls of tin, timber, and thatch nestled close together and, at this early hour, were already crowded with people and bright with colored cloths, fruits, vegetables, and Coca Cola signs. I was dispensable after all and just now, I needed the freedom to leave.

"Yes," I said, "John will look after the parish."

A seat was available on the day-flight to Paris and I boarded in the mid-afternoon. The plane roared down the tarmac and banked up into the clear blue sky, circling the city before it turned northward toward the equator.

A television screen showed the position of the airplane as it moved fractionally over the surface of the earth. Through the window, I watched the green-and-brown world that was represented by the TV map. We moved along the huge gash of the Rift Valley with its lakes strung out like beads.

Was this what it would be like for Dad? I wondered. The soul soaring free above the clouds. Light as air. Reaching up toward Heaven. If he had earned Heaven. I thought about the dull, routine existence that he loved to the exclusion of all things spiritual.

Looking out the window, I saw the snowy peaks of the great mountain as it rose majestically above the clouds that habitually shielded it from the eyes of the people below. Yes, Heaven must be something like this—the seeing of things unseen—the knowing of things unknown.

Flying had never frightened me. If the plane were to crash, I reasoned, that would mean I would never have to go back to the life down there. It would be like breaking free. Fanciful thoughts, maybe, but I allowed them because they soothed me and bore my spirits up on every flight I took.

Across the aisle from me, there were several children accompanied by two women draped in black robes. Only the women's brown eyes showed above the cloths that covered their faces.

The cabin crew came round with drinks and dinner. One of the children was receiving special treatment. There was a lot of to-ing and fro-ing. Whispered instructions. The hostess came back with a meal that looked substantially different to the others.

A fussy child, I thought, until I looked at the little

lad as he sat solemnly eating. Although he was only about seven or eight years old, he had an aura about him. Then I noticed how the women and even the other, older children addressed him with respect and a certain shyness. He must be a prince. A prince or a religious leader. And I marveled that a child's role in life could, so early, be determined and accepted.

I thought of myself at a similar age. How I had decided then what my life would be and how I had let no one deter me. Not even my father.

Did this boy have a choice? Absorbed in the question, I did not realize I was staring until those huge, knowing eyes locked on to mine and he smiled a serene smile.

My eyes flinched away from his gaze as I recognized his natural sense of superiority. This child and his role in life were indistinguishable, regardless of whether that role was chosen or decreed. For an instant, I envied him.

After the remains of dinner were cleared away, the television switched to the in-flight film, but I couldn't concentrate. The little lad across the aisle wasn't interested, either. I saw him curl up and sleep with his thumb in his mouth. Only then did the women loosen the veils across their mouths to talk quietly together. Out of their pockets they produced small quantities of food which they nibbled. They hadn't eaten any of the airplane food.

Below us the Sahara crawled by, hour after empty

hour. My thoughts turned, reluctantly but inevitably, to Ireland and my father.

"Duty free, sir?"

Startled out of my reveries, I replied: "Yes. A bottle of Irish whiskey and a cherry brandy, please." As I stowed the bag under the seat in front, I remembered: It was unlikely that Dad would ever drink this whiskey. Well, I would bring it to him anyway, as a gesture. Besides, there was a sneaking suspicion in my head that Dad would never just give up and die. He was far too dedicated to living. This was just a false alarm, I told myself. He would live to see his bottle emptied: pouring out full tumblers for his guests and leaving them no room to add water.

That thought carried me through the rest of my journey. In Paris, the little prince was escorted away to another flight. He moved regally in the company of his entourage, without so much as a glance at me.

Maybe it was my suspicion that Dad's condition had been exaggerated that left me so unprepared for the reality. The man in the bed was a shadow of the father I had known. Barely recognizable. His skin was stretched taut across the bones of his face. The false teeth (which my mother had always complained were smaller than his original teeth) were far too big in his shrunken face. His handshake was feeble, his eyes already dull.

"Hello, Dad."

His head made a scant nod of greeting.

"How are you?" What was I doing asking these questions? What did I expect him to say—fine? Dying? He said nothing. I was finding my role as son uncomfortable. What could I do, take him in my arms and hug him? He was my father, after all. But we had never been demonstrative. The closest I had ever got was once, in a boat, when the sea had rocked me off balance and I had clung to his leg for support. He had been big and strong then. If I hugged him now, I felt I would crush him.

So, I reverted to the role of priest. I gave him a blessing and saw disapproval in his eyes. "Will I give you absolution?"

"I've lived a good life," he said. His words were patient. Barely audible. Laborious. "Not blameless, but good enough. And I've known love in a way you never have."

"Perhaps human love is not enough."

"I don't need this . . ."

He closed his eyes and seemed to sleep. I kept vigil in the hope that he would speak to me again. This time, this time, I would say all the right things.

The scene reflected in my mother's dressing table mirror. My father dying in the bed. The blank square on the wall where he had insisted that my mother remove the picture of the Sacred Heart. Me sitting in the chair. I noticed that I was wearing the clerical collar that he despised. As a concession, I removed it and took his shrunken hand in mine. His eyes remained closed.

I was dozing, jetlagged, drifting in and out of reality, when I realized my father's breathing had changed. My mother was in the room. She bent to kiss his mouth. Then, she called Oonagh and they went on their knees beside him. Mother's hands, joined in prayer, held his hand tightly between them.

"Go on," she prompted. "The Last Rites."

"I'm not sure it's what he wants."

"It's what he needs," she said softly, "whether he knows it or not." She handed me my collar. My prayers were the words that accompanied him on his journey.

After he was gone, I went down to the bathroom, lifted the wooden seat and peed. The stream of urine hit the back of the toilet. Did my father ever notice that word, Twyford? Did he ever aim the jet of his pee to cover it? Did he ever think, as he buttoned up his fly and turned to wash his hands in the hand basin, that there would be a day when all of these things would be here without him and the mirror would be lonely for his reflection? It's not the mirror, it is I who am empty, I acknowledged.

Mum was in the bedroom, tidying. Organizing candles. Fussing, dry-eyed, brisk, efficient. This woman who had never coped, who had been cosseted and guarded by my father through the emotional roller coaster that her life became after the death of her unborn child.

"Can I help you?"

"I'm grand." She flashed me a brave smile. "He would have wanted me to be strong, like he was for me."

It rained that evening, as the undertakers came. I stood in the porch, watching the sky brightening through the filtering leaves as the shower subsided. I longed for the tropics. For the smell of soil and vegetation rising on the warm air. White ants on the wing flapping in their hundreds round the porch light.

The old porch had been renovated in white PVC and the leaky roof had been replaced. One of the many renovations that Oonagh and her husband had made since they had moved in. It had been assumed, without asking, that the house would be left to Oonagh. And so it should be. What use had I for it?

I thought for a moment about how much money a place like this was worth. And what that money could do to alleviate suffering in Kishagi. But the thought seemed disloyal to the family. Oonagh's children were growing up here, just as I had. She and they were welcome to our mother's house. I was the one who had opted out.

The undertakers didn't ask for my help. My mother was giving directions. He wouldn't have been a one for gold handles, I thought, as they shouldered the ornate wooden coffin through the hallway. Someone stumbled on the step and the coffin bumped against the hall door. Where the paint chipped, I saw a streak of green on the door underneath. I was strangely pleased to see it, because, in my memory, that door had always been green. And I remembered once arguing with Oonagh who claimed it had always been red. Although one time, when I was a child, I had found a sun-blister on the paint and had squeezed it with my fingernail so that the blister split and rippled and I saw layers of other colors underneath—colors I had never known. It pleased me, somehow, to know that my memory was not wrong, and that it was still the same door. The same door knocker, too—a fist holding a laurel wreath. How many times had my father raised that wreath in his hand? I wondered (Dad was always forgetting his keys—maybe as a stalling tactic to give Mum time to collect herself when he came home, I used to think. Although he always arrived at the same time exactly—twenty past six.) How many layers of his skin had he left on that knocker? I wondered. Dead skin from a hand now also dead. The door had outlived him, the knocker, the house, the green paint. He came here as a bridegroom to my mother's house and he left now as silently and as empty-handed as he had come.

I didn't shoulder my father's coffin. Instead, I stood, dressed in alb and chasuble, waiting at the altar steps with my brothers in Christ. The body of my father, in its box with the gold handles, was brought to rest before me. I blessed it with holy water.

"Receive his soul and present it to God, present his soul to God most high," sang the choir.

Most of the funeral passed me by in a blur of unexpected grief, in biting my lip to control the tell-tale quivering. But there were flashes of stark clarity. The faces of the congregation. How strange that they should all be white. Glimpses of the tear-streaked faces of my mother and sister in the front row. Familiar but different. Connected to me through the past. Beloved but estranged.

I was irritated by a young altar boy scratching his ear. A little altar girl giggling. An old priest fumbling his prayers and forgetting the words. What is happening to this ritual, I wondered? This sacrament of the Eucharist which had drawn me, as a child, in all its smooth perfection of grace and movement. It had become sloppy and shoddy. On that day, of all days, when it should have been perfect for the funeral of my father.

The readings and sermon were delivered from the simple wooden lectern on the altar. Not from the pulpit; I was glad of that. Dad was always ranting on about that pulpit. It had its own carved spire reaching up toward the soaring heights of the cathedral roof. And steps leading up to the space where the priest stood, elevated and framed by this elegance. Punch and Judy, my father had called it. To create the illusion of the priest as a puppet with God pulling his strings. Out of the corner of my eye, I sought the source of another peeve. The bishop's carved chair, intricately crafted. "Because his Lordship couldn't plonk his arse on a wooden bench the same as the rest of us." I heard my father's words as if he were beside me. The bishop had not graced us with his presence today. I was glad of that, too.

My maternal grandfather, a runaway schoolboy, had arrived here by train, paying his fare with a shilling he had found on the street. He had signed on as an apprentice stone carver on this cathedral. It was a source of family pride on my mother's side, but quietly scoffed at by my father. For a minute, I could see that young boy hewing away at those huge hunks of brown marble that became the bases of the pillars. Sculpting out the curlicues in the brown marble canopy above the pulpit. Kneeling on the floor, sticking down all those colored quarter-inch tiles that made up the mosaic floor. Sandpapering the bishop's chair. I saw the great windows open to the sky, awaiting their stained glass. Heard the noise of drills and hammers; the voices ringing out irreverently above the din; the laughter and the crude jokes in this place before it was consecrated.

My grandfather used to say that, high up on their scaffoldings, beyond the reach of the foreman's eyes, the sculptors carved out their own personal works of art during their lunch breaks. If anyone were to climb up that high, he would find unseen treasures hidden beneath the roof.

The cathedral had been built for quite a while before the spire was added. The budget must have been squandered on the ornate interior. I had seen photographs of the cathedral without its spire. It seemed odd and squat. Like an enormous frog crouched and ready to spring. Gigantic, even then, compared to the scale of the buildings round it. The site itself was elevated on a huge parapet. The spire added stability and aspirations.

It made the cathedral the largest and most magnificent building in the town, overshadowing its Protestant rivals in a great statement of Catholic emancipation.

Its glorious bells were installed and rang out across the rooftops and the bay, marking the hours and the quarter hours. People timed their watches to those bells, subconsciously hastening or slowing their steps in response to their toll. Fishermen in the harbor threw out another net or hauled one in, according to the rhythm of their chime. And businesspeople waited for their signal to tell them when to open or close.

As a child, I would sit on the steps with my mother as those bells rang out their sweet melodies, sacred and secular. If you stood below and looked right up at the cross on the top of the spire, you would think that it was the spire and not the clouds behind that moved. And it seemed as if the spire was tumbling down on top of you. I used to look at it for so long that my head would spin and I would have to sit down.

But for this cathedral, my grandfather would not have come to the town and stayed to become a prosperous and respected businessman. He would never have met my grandmother. Neither my mother nor I would exist. It shocked me that my father could dismiss all his beautiful stonework as "cake decoration."

Then I thought about the simple structure that was the church of Kishagi. It had open block-work instead of windows and the only decoration was a mural by a

local artist. It depicted a black Christ on the cross and a
bug-eyed black angel. For a strange, dizzying moment, I
dreamt of bringing my father's body there. It would
have suited him better than this vastly over-indulgent
extravagance of carved marble and mosaic.

It struck me that my father, being dead, would now
become part of a heavenly squinting gallery, knowing
my thoughts and deeds. Already, he was infiltrating my
thoughts.

The people from the front seats were filing up for
communion. I noticed Oonagh sitting back in her seat
as her husband and children squeezed past her and up
to the altar rails. As I dished out the hosts into the
waiting hands and mouths of the congregation, I looked
again and again in her direction, but she wouldn't catch
my eye.

Although I added my own voice to the prayers of
comfort for the bereaved, I could find no solace in them
for myself. My father had died. He was in Heaven, they
said, reaping the just rewards of an exemplary life. But
what if he wasn't? What if his stubborn anti-Catholic
attitudes excluded him from paradise? I found myself
in a fretful state, thinking of my own shortcomings.
How I strove and strove for perfection of spirit and how
I failed constantly. And if my spiritual striving left me
so unworthy, how much less worthy was he, who lived
all his life so solidly attached to the earth and the things
of the earth? As the clods fell on the coffin and the

Hail Marys resounded across the cemetery, my heart palpitated in fear for this man, this father.

People came and shook my hand. "He was a saint," one of my father's friends said.

"He was." I agreed because I couldn't let him down.

"Are you still out there in Africa?" an old neighbor asked. "And tell me, are they all darkies out there now, Father? And aren't you the great man to be working with the likes of them." I didn't know what to say to him. Whatever I said, it would not be enough to ever penetrate his ignorance.

A friend of my mother's told me how proud my father always was of me. She kept holding my hand as she spoke. "And isn't it such a blessing for your Mammy to have a priest in the family." It embarrassed me, this strange, fawning familiarity. "I'll do the nine first Fridays for your poor Daddy." The thought that had been bothering me was suddenly obscene when insinuated in her words. I turned away from her, aghast. Looking around, then, at the people of my own home town, I knew myself to be a stranger in their midst.

At the graveyard gates was a rough-looking man with bloodshot eyes and unkempt hair. He shambled toward me as I emerged. "We know what ye bastards were at all the years," he said. "We knows it all now."

The undertaker shouted at him: "Get on ourra that now, Paddy, have some respect for the dead." The man looked back at me with his red, resentful eyes. I was glad to reach the sanctuary of my sister's car.

We waited for Mum to finish with the handshaking and the condolences. It was the first chance I had got to talk to Oonagh on her own. "Why didn't you tell me that Dad was ill?"

She was busy, checking messages on her mobile phone.

"Oonagh?"

She looked at me as if I had only just asked. As if I was unreasonable in expecting her to answer sooner. "He didn't want us to tell you."

"But . . ."

"He didn't want you interfering in his dying."

"You should have told me just the same."

"And gone against his wishes? Anyway, he was right. You *would* have interfered."

I opened my mouth to protest, but arguing with Oonagh was always as fruitless as arguing with my father himself. "So, how long was he sick?"

"Six months, maybe. Six weeks since we heard." Oonagh was adjusting the car mirror, inspecting her makeup.

"Wasn't there any possibility of saving him?"

"It was too late."

"But why didn't he do something about it earlier?"

"He was philosophical about dying. Didn't want medical intervention." Her voice was muffled as she pursed her lips and applied a coat of lipstick. "His time was up, that was all. It was the way he wanted it."

"Of all the stupid, stubborn old . . ."

She turned from the mirror to interrupt me and her eyes were sparkling with unshed tears. "I think he was rather brave. And if you don't stop at me, I'll have to do this makeup all over again."

"You didn't go to communion."

"No."

"Why?"

"None of your business. But seeing as it bothers you—I'm an atheist."

"After himself."

"Uh-oh." She lifted the mascara brush from her eyelashes to shake her head vehemently. "Dad was a solid believer. A very spiritual man. His problem was with the trappings of Catholicism. The circus, as he called it. And your involvement in that."

"A circus? Jesus, Oonagh, is that what he thought of what I'm at?"

"Yeah. But I wouldn't take it too much to heart. You're entitled to believe in whatever you do. Just so long as you don't expect the rest of us to do the same. Or grovel." She smiled for the first time.

"I'm glad, Oonagh, that you don't grovel to anyone. That you're so like him."

"And you're like us too, if you'd see it."

The news that night showed a queue of refugees outside the immigration office. An African man was interviewed. "I have been coming here for weeks, now," he said.

"The Irish priests and nuns tell us that this is a good place where we will be welcome. But it is not like that."

A church was burned in Northern Ireland that weekend. The television coverage showed a priest emerging from the still-smoldering building. He was carrying clear plastic bags containing priceless gold chalices and patens, which he had rescued from the safe after the blaze. He didn't seem happy to be photographed as he hurried into a waiting car. "Look at your man," my father whispered in my ear. "Escaping with the loot."

"Isn't it desperate?" my mother said. For a second I thought that she was echoing my father's sentiments. "In the name of all that's good and holy, how could anyone desecrate a church? Is nothing sacred anymore? And all these scandals!" She shook her head sadly.

His voice was in my ear again, not whispering this time, but on a favorite tirade: "The priests with their blackthorn sticks rooting the couples out of the ditches. Concerning themselves where they had no place, in the private lives of others. 'Twas because they never had a woman themselves that they took such a keen interest. In the confession boxes drooling over the sins." His rant was tame in the light of recent revelations of sexual liaisons and child abuse.

I touched my mother's hand. It felt cold and dry-skinned. "I feel guilty. As if, by being a priest, I am in some way an accomplice to those abuses and abusers. It's the same way I feel about being white in Africa. As if somehow I am to blame for all of the atrocities committed in my name by other white people." She didn't understand. I didn't expect her to. It was something I could barely fathom myself, this shame that I carried with me for my race and my cloth. "I wish, Mother, that we could go back to the simple way it was."

"It wasn't ever that simple," my father shouted. "'Twas all whitewash."

I squeezed my mother's cold, dry hand. "I'm sorry. Sorry that the safe Catholic world you knew wasn't all you thought it was. But our trust is in God, not in men."

A telephone is ringing somewhere in the house. I presume someone will answer it, but no one does. Has Shiku gone out and left me on my own? A flicker of fear passes through me. What if someone knows I'm here? The ringing persists and leaves me anxious, unable to work. I decide to go and take the telephone off the hook.

The phone is on a small table in the dining room. By the time I shuffle to it, it has stopped ringing. Breathless, I sit down on the upholstered seat beside it. I lift the receiver to take it off the hook, then a thought comes to me. I slip my finger into the digit ring and dial 00353. I pause. The call clicks through international. I feel a kind of relief. As if the real world might have changed. I chuckle to myself as I complete the number. Why had I not thought of this?

"Hello?"

"Oonagh, it's Ciarán."

"Oh, thank God! We've been worried sick."

"Didn't anyone ring you?"

"We got some garbled message about you being injured. Some Father . . . Madden, I think it was . . . rang.
I'm afraid I wasn't very polite to him."

"You couldn't be rude enough to that shagger."

She stopped. Sniggered. "Is this my beloved brother
the saint?"

"Maybe not so saintly."

"I kind of gathered that. That there was a bit of a . . .
scandal? I had a notion of you being defrocked!" she
laughed. With relief as well as humor, I realized. "He
said you had been injured but wouldn't tell me anymore.
So, I told him if he couldn't give me proper information
he wasn't to be ringing up here alarming us all. I told
him I didn't want my mother to be told anything."

"You mean Mother doesn't know?"

"No. Sure, how could I pass on that worry to her
when the shagger, as you call him, wouldn't tell me
anything?"

"Oonagh, you're wonderful." I remembered the silence around my father's illness.

"I told Mum you had rung when she was out and
that you had a bout of your malaria. Not to alarm her
too much. And then I rang your superiors; they weren't
giving out any information over the phone. I sensed
some kind of scandal."

"Intrigue rather than scandal."

"Mother was upset that you never rang for Christmas. Did you get our cards?"

"No. I haven't been back to Kishagi. I couldn't phone at Christmas. I was semiconscious. In hospital."

"Sweet Christ! Are you all right?"

"Yeah. I'm okay now."

"What happened?"

"Some fella had a go at me with a machete. Messy, but not fatal, fortunately."

"That's something, by the sounds of it. Will I put you on to Mum?"

"No. Just tell her I rang when she was out." I'm feeling too tired, now. If I speak to my mother, I'll weep. "Oonagh?"

"Yes?"

"I love you, Oonagh."

"Yeah. I love you, too, Ciarán. You mind yourself now, won't you?"

"Yeah."

As I put down the phone I hear a sound and look up to see Muthoni standing quietly watching me. "Now you can come out of your room, you can come and see Sungura in the garden."

"Not today. This . . ." I look ruefully at the few short steps between my bedroom door and the place where I am sitting. "This much has me exhausted. I am not so very strong."

"I will help you," she says. "Today, you come to

here. Tomorrow, we go to there." She points down some steps to a sitting room on a lower level. "The next day, we go outside to the patio. And the day after that, we see Sungura. I will tell him you are coming to visit."

"Okay. Nurse Esther tells me I must walk. So, I'll walk with you. Where's your mother?"

"She is gone to get books and things for going back to school. The ayah went to the quarters to drink tea with her friend. We can ring the bell, but we don't need her. You can lean on me."

Muthoni takes me confidently by the hand and I struggle to my feet. We make slow progress to the bedroom. I lean my weight away from her small, supportive frame. Her courage and her energy are like a tonic. We even climb together up the three steps to my little alcove before the mirror. She skips back down the steps and turns to wag a finger at me. "Tomorrow."

"Tomorrow." I don't ever remember being so pleasantly bullied.

10

Every day for a week now, I have climbed the three steps to my desk to write my memoirs. Each morning I close the mirrors to avoid seeing my reflection. But the nurse, or Shiku, constantly reopens them. This morning, they are open when I arrive. One of the images that spooks me is the two side mirrors reflecting their reflection infinitely. I cannot think of such distances, such times. My life has become finite.

"You always knew your life was finite," my death's head tells me.

"Yes," I say, "but with the promise of Heaven."

"It *was* Heaven," he reminds me.

"Yes, but it wasn't eternal, it stopped."

"It did, this time," he answers back.

Maybe I'm becoming less afraid, because this morning he seems less threatening. I look at him squarely. There is a little color in his white cheeks. His eyes are not so dead as I remember. I feel my cheeks and watch my reflection do the same. Perhaps I will learn to live with this new, estranged self. Or maybe he is fooling me. To distract me from my task: this essential work of recreating my own life. I move the mirrors so that I can see all three sides. I can see the back of my own head with a bald patch at the crown, as if I had been tonsured like a monk. The image pleases me. It suits the feeling of my cell. I decide to work with the mirrors open.

Once, my father brought me on a "mystery tour." Usually, on our outings together, we gathered up our lines and rods, traces and feathers, and drove down to the harbor where Dad kept his fishing boat. But, that day, we went on a longer jaunt. The old Morris Minor carried us along the twisty ribbons of West Cork Road, up and down and round until we came in sight of the sea—startling blue and the islands, green and gray.

"Are we going on a big ship? Or is it small like a *currach*?"

"Medium," he answered. "And there's a surprise for you when we get to where we're going."

He parked the car on a stone pier with round bollards for tying up boats. "That's her," he said, pointing.

Why did he call boats and cars "her"? I wondered.

"She" was like a trawler—a floating tub. He took my hand as we climbed down slippery steps.

"Look, can you see what's written on her side?" he asked.

There were three words painted in white letters on

the hull. I recognized the middle one. My own name—
Ciarán.

"*Naomh Ciarán Corcaigh,*" he translated: "The Saint
Ciarán—Cork, because that's where we are."

"Is it called after me, Dad?"

"After Saint Ciarán. We named you after him," he
said, lifting me aboard.

Dad and another man chatted in Irish as the waves
plash-plashed beneath us and the boat sped out among
the islands. He stood solidly on deck, his legs spread to
counteract the buffeting of the boat. Beside him, I was
almost rocked off my feet at times and had to cling to
his leg for support. The wind caught the tails of his
khaki overcoat and I leaned close against him, smelling
the salty smell of the cloth and plucking at his sleeve.
"What's the surprise, Dad? Tell me." He just smiled and
put his finger to his lips.

"There it is," Dad said as the boat passed by a hump-
backed island.

"Why are we going past it?"

"We're not." As he spoke I felt the boat turning and
we churned the water round us as the walls of the harbor seemed to draw back to make way for us. We pulled
up at the foot of a stone pier.

My name was everywhere on that island. The harbor
was Ciarán's harbor and the strand was Ciarán's strand.
We cupped our hands and drank from Ciarán's well.

"This spring never dries up," Dad told me. "Though
it runs so close to the tide, it's always fresh water."

It was springtime and primroses were blooming in ditches. Robins hopped from stone to stone and the air was filled with birdsong. We trudged together up the steep hill to the pub, where Dad tapped a coin on the counter for service. There was a step in the doorway between the bar and the room behind—a stone step that had been worn by the walking of feet. How many foot-steps had it taken to wear it away like that? I tried to think numbers: thousands, millions, billions, trillions. The pub owner came out and I watched his foot brush the step, doing its own tiny piece of destruction. I tried to think smallness: teeny, weeny, weenchy. Could a speck of stone be light enough to float like dust in the air?

The face of the barman beamed over the counter at me and his large hand clasped mine warmly. He with-drew and returned with gifts—a glass of bubbling lem-onade and a bar of chocolate "for the little maneen."

We sat outside on a bench and watched a small tri-angle of shimmering blue sea in a V between two hills. My father wiped a white moustache of froth from his lip and, settling his pint on the ground between his big shoes, relaxed into a story:

"Your saint, Ciarán, was a young boy once like you are. Before he was born, his mother had a vision that a star had fallen into her mouth. She went to the druids—the wise men that were around at that time—and asked them what the dream meant. They said to her: 'You'll give birth to a marvelous son and great will be his character and his virtues to the end of the world.'

"After that, Ciarán was born here on this island. One day while he was only a young child, a great kite came and hovered over his head. Then it swooped down on a little sparrow that was lying in its nest. Ciarán was moved to pity as he watched the tiny, defenseless creature being pecked and torn asunder. But suddenly, the bird of prey came back and laid the little bird, half dead, at Ciarán's feet. He lifted the sparrow in his hands and his tears flowed and mingled with the blood on the bird's feathers. And the sparrow was made whole again and flew to its nest.

"Ciarán spent thirty years in perfection of body and soul. There were no Christians at that time, only pagans in all of Ireland. But there were some men who came in a boat and told him about Christianity being in Rome. And away Ciarán went and got baptized there. He stayed in Rome for twenty years, reading the Scriptures before he was ordained a priest.

"On his way back to Ireland, who did he meet on the road but St. Patrick himself. 'Go on before me,' St. Patrick said, 'and in the middle of Ireland you'll find a well. That's where you must found your monastery.'

"'But,' Ciarán asked, 'how will I know if I'm at the right place?'

"'Take this bell,' St. Patrick said. ''Twon't ring until you get there.'

"Ciarán took the little bell that made no sound. It was silent all the way until he reached that spot, in the very center of Ireland, between the north and south. Then the bell suddenly rang out with a bright melodious sound, and he knew he had found the right place.

"He sat down in the shade of a tree and a fierce wild pig sprang up out of the bushes beside him. It eyed Ciarán and fled, but came back a while later and was a gentle servant to him. That pig was the first disciple Ciarán had."

Dad drained his pint and took my hand as we set off back to the harbor. "I know, I know," he said. "It's a bit farfetched, but not a bad yarn for all that. A badger and a wolf came to Ciarán and were submissive to him. Then, one day, a fox came. He was clever and bad. He sneaked into Ciarán's cell and stole his sandals. By the time the badger chased him and found him in his den, he had eaten the shoes, lugs and thongs, and all.

"Eventually, the fox came back to Ciarán and begged him to forgive him. From then on, he was holy, like all the others."

"Dad? Why did Ciarán preach to animals? Weren't there any people living in that place?"

"I suppose St. Patrick wanted to keep the important business for himself. Ciarán wasn't that great a saint. He was only the harbinger."

"What's that?"

"The one who goes before."

As we spoke, we had climbed over a stile and there, among the gravestones, were the ruins of an old stone building.

"Or maybe Ciarán was only practicing on the animals," Dad replied. "Because afterward he came back to Cléire and converted all the people here. This is his church."

The stone gable and tumbledown walls were covered in moss and lichen. There was the earthy smell of decay.

"Were they teenchy people that time, Dad?"

"No," he said, "it's just the ground has built up around it, over hundreds and hundreds of years."

I nodded sagely, thinking of all those tiny particles of stone from the step and where they might settle. "How many hundreds?"

"Fifteen."

Fifteen hundred years. That was the same as one thousand five hundred. I touched the stone of the ruined church and felt the burden of that weight of years and, through them, I felt connected way back to those ancient times and to my saint—a boy like me. I felt the power of that ancient story running through my bones. I felt, suddenly, very old and very young and very small, all at the same time.

"What's wrong with you, Ciarán? Have you seen a ghost?" my father asked.

I had not the words to tell him what had happened to me.

***

"Bwana Ciarán?" Muthoni's voice interrupts me. "This time we go for a walk. Yes?"

"Yes." I am tired from writing.

Shiku laughs at our slow baby steps across the parquet floor of the dining room. I grasp the banister on the steps to the lower level. By the time we reach the sitting room couch, Shiku has brought a tray of tea and biscuits as a reward for our efforts.

"Are there stories where you come from, Bwana Ciarán?"

"Lots of stories."

"About the animals? Tell me one about them."

"Well, once upon a time there was a man called Ciarán."

"Like you."

"Yes, like me. And he was a priest, like me. Only this was a long, long time ago. And he met a great saint called Patrick."

"What's a saint?"

"A holy man. And Patrick told Ciarán to go to the very middle of my country, and that there he would find a well. And when Ciarán found that place, the first person he met there was a pig. And then he met a badger."

"What's a badger?"

"He's a small animal. About the size of a dog. But fatter, maybe more like a pig but with stripy fur."

"Not big like an elephant."

"No. We don't have elephants."

"Hippos?"

"No hippos."

"Rhinoceroses?"

"No."

"Snakes?"

"No. St. Patrick, the holy man, sent all the snakes away."

"Ah. I would like to live where you come from, bwana Ciarán. Me, I do not like those snakes."

"Snakes are all right, Muthoni. Most of them aren't poisonous. And anyway, they usually only bite you when you disturb them. But if you make big, loud footsteps they'll run away."

"Do you like snakes, bwana Ciarán?"

"What I really admire about them is the way they shed their skins, leave their old life behind and move on, all new and shiny. The holy man in my story didn't like snakes because they could do that. He wanted everyone to follow his way. So snakes didn't fit into his plan."

"Are there *sunguras* where you come from?"

"Yes. We have rabbits. And we have hares. Even our own special one called the Irish hare. He is like this one in the story, I think. And a *sungura* came to Ciarán and was his devoted servant. Not a slave, like that *sungura*. He stayed there because he wanted to be there and he wanted to pray to Ciarán's god."

"Ngai."

"Yes, the Christian Ngai, the father of Jesus. And one day, a fox came and he was wicked and bad. He sneaked into Ciarán's cell in the middle of the night and stole his sandals.

"Ciarán sent the badger to find the fox and when he got to the fox's den, it was too late, the sandals were eaten. But after that, the fox came back and was a good friend to Ciarán."

"Why?"

"Why what?"

"Why did the fox come back? What did Ciarán say to him?"

"Oh." There was a childish turn in the story that I had dismissed and forgotten years ago, but Muthoni had sensed its lack.

"He said to the fox: 'If God had wanted you to eat meat, he would have made meat grow on those trees there.' So, not only did the fox agree to live a holy Christian life, but afterward he never ate meat again."

"What did he eat?"

"Vegetables, I suppose. Grass maybe."

Muthoni thinks seriously for a second. Then she says, very dismissively: "No. A fox cannot be a vegetarian. A fox must eat meat. It is what he was meant to do."

"I agree with you, Muthoni." And suddenly I see the sting in the tail of the story. The forgotten part of the

deal—the part that made me spend my whole life denying my own nature.

"Does meat grow on trees where you live?"

"No."

"What does?"

"Like here. Leaves. Flowers. Fruit."

"Avocados? Bananas? Mangoes?"

"Not those kind of fruits. Apples. Pears. Cherries.
Peaches."

"Do you have pineapples? Oranges? Tea? Coffee?"

"We can buy them, but they don't grow there."

"Ah bwana Ciarán, there are many things missing
where you come from."

Shiku, who has been sitting quietly, half listening
with a look of amusement in her eyes, now laughs out-
right.

"You are so right, Muthoni," she says, "Ciarán has
had many things missing in his life." And she gives me
a wicked and unmistakable wink.

Next day, the glass doors are open and Muthoni, Shiku,
and I sit outside on an octagonal patio with pillars and
a high, timbered roof. The jacaranda trees are in their
second blooming. Bougainvillea sprouts wildly in a lower
section of the garden, down steps. Busy Lizzies make a
splash of color in the flower beds. Insects hum and
hornbills screech in the trees. A monkey comes crash-
ing through the branches.

"I had forgotten how beautiful it all is."

"Ah," Shiku apologizes, "you are not seeing my garden at its best. The gardener has gone away."

"I wouldn't prefer it any other way."

At last, Muthoni brings me to the rabbit hutch where Sungura pauses in his nibbling and digging to sniff at our fingers through the chicken-wire fence. There is a sense of fulfillment in having reached here. This child has challenged me and made me overcome my reluctance to go outside. Because of her, I have taken strides forward in my recovery. She picks a bunch of flowers that have to be brought back to my room and put in water on my "desk." I am left there with my sprigs of bougainvillea and a reminder that, tomorrow, we will see Sungura again.

Each day we go a little farther, exploring the garden. The rabbit is let out to hop around our feet. When Shiku isn't looking, Muthoni feeds him biscuits as we drink our tea on the patio.

This evening, Shiku invites me down to the sitting room after dinner. She has swapped her "school clothes" for a long, elaborate dress in green cloth with pink and purple flowers. As she swishes past me and throws open the patio doors, I imagine that the scent, her scent, emanates from those colorful cloth flowers. There is a high color in her cheeks. A brightness in her eyes. A lightness in her step as she carries two glasses and a bottle of wine outside to the warm darkness. She lights

some candles and their flickering glow shows her in
silhouette as she pours out the wine.

"Come on," she invites. "Are you going to sit in
there on your own?"

I shamble self-consciously out to the patio. "I thought
you were expecting guests."

"You are my guest. You are my birthday party.
Cheers."

I raise my glass to her. The wine is red. It reminds
me of altar wine. "Happy birthday, Shiku. I'm afraid
I'm a dull companion for a party."

She presents her cheeks to me to be kissed three
times: the right, the left, the right.

There is only one seat on the patio. We sit close
together.

"I am not going to miss Julius tonight. I swear it."
She clinks her glass against mine as if we have made a
pact.

"I don't know how he can go off and leave you for
so long."

She smiles. Touches my sleeve. "It is okay. Soon, he
will finish his doctorate and he will come home. Besides, I am not lonely with you here." But as she looks
away toward the garden, the loneliness is there in her
face. I feel an ache in my heart. For her. For me.

"If you were mine I wouldn't ever leave your side.
Not for a minute."

She looks slightly embarrassed but laughs it off.

"Then who would do the work? Who would earn the money?"

I let the crowding emotions subside as I watch her skillfully steer the conversation away to safer topics.

"Was it that story that made you become a priest? Did you want to be a saint, like St. Ciarán?" She cannot hide the hint of mockery in her voice.

"Maybe. But my mother was a very pious woman; that was part of it, too."

"Was she happy when you told her you had a calling?"

"It was strange. I remember she was in the drawing room that day. There was always a smell of polish and camphor in there. But, that day, there was a smell of knitting wool and of dusty sunshine through the window. My mother was sitting with her hands on her lap. The knitting needles and wool were on the small table—blue wool. I remember noticing that she hadn't knitted any of it for weeks. She would go broody, sometimes, my mother, away off in her own little world.

"'Mammy,'" I said.

"'Mmm?' she answered.

"There wasn't a question. I just needed to say her name. To wake her out of whatever dream it was that kept her there so silent, so apart from me.

"'Can I have sixpence?'

"'What for?'

"'For . . . for nothing.'

"She'd spoken, she'd moved. She'd noticed I was there, but nothing had changed.

"'Mammy?'

"'Yes?'

"'When I grow up . . .'

"'Yes, love?'

"'When I grow up, I want to go to Africa and tell the children there about Jesus, so they can be happy like I am.'

"'That's nice, love. Are you happy?'

"'Well, yes. Amn't I?'

"'I suppose so. You're lucky.'

"'Isn't Baby Declan lucky to be in Heaven? Isn't he happy?'

"'Ah yes. But not like you are.'

Shiku smiles at my recollections. "Ah yes, your little angel brother. You have mentioned him in sermons. I was always so intrigued." The perfume wafts out with each sweep of her hand as she illustrates her speech with gestures. "But, where did you, as a child, get the idea that you should come to Africa?"

"Father Madden came to our school and showed us a film about the missionaries in a place called—Barawana, I think it was. They were building a school. And it was the first time I had seen African people. I believed that the children were happy because they had been told about Jesus."

"You mean it was that racist who influenced you to come here?"

"I apologize for him, Shiku. Please don't confuse my attitude with his. I was eight years old. Even then, I should have seen through him. There was something in the way he shook my hand, holding it too long, rolling and squeezing it between his fingers. 'And now, Keerin, so you think you might be a special boy, chosen by God.' And I told him that my name wasn't Keerin, it was Ciarán. And he said: 'Ah, but the saint was Keerin, wasn't he?' And I said no, that the Saint was Ciarán and that he had a strand called after him and a church and a boat and that I was called after him, too. If I'd ever thought about it logically, as an adult, I think I would have seen what he was."

"Ciarán . . . I remember something you told me once. You said that Kishagi was in the very center of the world, between the north and south and that when you came there the church bell was ringing, so you knew that you had found the right place. What was that about?"

"That's part of the same story. St. Ciarán founded his monastery in the very center of Ireland, between the north and south. And when he entered that place, St. Patrick's bell, the one that had been silent, rang out loudly and clearly."

"So, it was really your father who made you become a priest."

I see her noticing my frown. "No. It wasn't my father. He was against my vocation."

"What did he say when you told him?"

"He said: 'Haven't we enough religious fanatics in this house without you starting?'"

Shiku laughs, and my reaction is annoyance, until I remember that she is right and that he was right to oppose me.

"'And Ciarán spent thirty years in perfection of body and spirit,'" I quote sadly.

"You were never even tempted?" she asks.

"Oh yes, I was tempted."

The wine is making her voluble. She chats about school and her students. Inconsequential things. Her face grows serious. "I love my job. I can never thank you . . ."

"My reasons for sending you away to boarding school were not so altruistic. I was afraid that I wouldn't be able to keep control over my feelings for you. I thought those feelings would subside when you went. But they didn't for a long time. I prayed for forgiveness. For direction. And when you came back with Julius, I felt my prayers had been answered. God, in his wisdom, had taken you away from me, beyond my reach, and simplified my life, while, at the same time, giving you happiness, wealth, security. And then I had to marry you to him. That was my penance. That was terrible. Though there was a strange kind of joy in it, too. Happiness that you'd found happiness. Spiritual satisfaction in losing you, if you know what I mean. I was regaining my spiritual freedom. Returning to my uncomplicated life, recommitting myself to my vocation."

She laughs a high, tinkling little laugh. "Ah, so I tempted you?"

"You don't know how hard you were to resist." I think about her perfume, wonder if she dabs it behind her ears, or on her wrists or in the creases of her elbows. Or if she bathes in it. "Do you know how beautiful you are?"

"You are trying to flatter me." Shiku's restless hand strokes my face, then flits down to rest, momentarily, on my elbow.

"It isn't flattery. It's truth." An insect flies into the candle and burns up in the flame.

The crickets fill the silence with their sawing. Shiku is quiet, too. She slips her hand into mine. I let my eyes move over her, noticing the tiniest little things, like the way her hair pulls free of the tight plait in which she wears it, and curls at the nape of her neck. I am glad that she doesn't wear hair extensions. On her, this traditional style is elegant.

"Do you remember the time I tried to kiss you?" she asks.

"I shouldn't have resisted. My life would have been worth something if I'd had you."

"You've been a great and a good man, always. Saintly, even."

"I've been much deluded, Shiku." I put my arm around her shoulders. "This is all we can be sure of, this life, this moment." I draw her in against me. "The two of us here on this patio."

She doesn't pull away, but takes my chin in her hand. "So, you will not resist me this time?"

Her lips mold my innocent lips into a kiss. The hairs tingle at the back of my neck. This long-forbidden moment is sweeter than I had ever thought it could be. Yet, it is free of desire, empty of the possibility of fulfillment. I hear her breath, stifled but heavy. A sigh escapes from her. I hold her body tighter, increase the pressure of my lips on hers. I will pander to her desire. I will tend to her passion. Satisfy her in whatever small way I can. But, suddenly, I am swooning beneath the moment, beneath her touch, beneath the rapture. I am lost. Drowning in the scent of her flowers.

A sound in the darkness makes her withdraw from me. Some nocturnal creature, in his ramblings, has cracked a twig beneath his paws. Or maybe it is the watchman making a tactful patrol around this scene.

The drink and the night and the kiss have all combined to make me brave or stupid. "I love you, Shiku."

A look of shock crosses her face. She says nothing. I persist.

"Tell me you love me."

"Maybe I did a small bit, when I was so young. But it was not like it is with . . ."

"Shhh." I touch my fingers to her lips. She pushes my hand away and straightens herself up, smoothing her dress.

That's enough. She does not say the words, maybe,

but I understand them. What has passed between us is still forbidden. Not by my code now, but by hers.

We pour out the last of the wine. She dawdles over it and I watch the way the candlelight sparkles in the glass as she raises it to her lips. There is animation in her voice. Small giggles intersperse her conversation. She is giddy from the drink but self-conscious with me now, I realize.

11

By now, I am well enough to venture into the garden on my own. And some afternoons, I take my notebook and my pen and sit on a bench beneath a jacaranda tree to write my memoirs.

One day, there was a terrible squawking from the stables at the back of the garden. I ran through briars and nettles to reach the old doorway. The roof of the stable had fallen in years ago and inside was as overgrown as the garden outside. Our cat came bounding through the bushes to me. He mewed and rubbed himself against my scratched and bleeding legs.

"Bold cat! What have you done?"

"What's wrong?" My father had heard the commotion and was standing in the threshold behind me.

"The cat got a bird. I think it's hurt."

Dad held back the tangles of briars and beat down nettles to make a path for me to squeeze through. A young jackdaw was lying shivering and screeching in the corner, one wing dangling useless, one leg broken, blood on his feathers where the cat had mauled him. His round gray eyes blinked with terror. He trembled in my hands as I brought him out.

"The poor thing," my father said, gently stroking its head.

Before I realized what he was doing, he had taken its neck between his big thumb and forefinger. There was a click as he snapped the tiny backbone. The jackdaw shuddered and was still.

I felt hot tears scalding my face. "What did you do that for? Didn't you know that I could have . . .?" I wanted to lunge at him, to beat him with my fists.

"You could have done what? Mended him? Ah, Ciarán, that's only old *pishogues!*"

Something between us was broken that day. He had denied the truth of his own story. Somehow, that made me more determined to follow the dream. To prove him wrong.

Dad drove me to the seminary in the Morris 1100 he had at that time. It was nineteen seventy-four and I was seventeen. My trunk, containing the new black soutane, black trousers and little else besides clothes, was packed and stowed in the boot. He kept his eye on the road as he always did, carefully not looking at me as he spoke.

"I really hoped you'd give up this nonsense."

"It's what I've always wanted to do. You know that."

"There's a whole world out there you haven't experienced. You don't even know what you're sacrificing."

"Sacrificing?"

"You've chosen a lonely life. I'd have wanted you to find a wife, to have a family."

"Like you have."

His jaw jutted forward and he took his eyes off the road for a long second to stare at me. "Like I have."

"Watch the road, Dad."

In the silence that followed, I noticed his hand white around the knuckles where he clasped the steering wheel. I watched ditches and houses streaming past. Why couldn't the old man understand? I would never settle for his mundane life—the tedious round of days at work and nights at home in front of the television. He could have all that. My calling was more noble. Of a higher order.

One of the first theological essays we were asked to write was on the Creation from the book of Genesis. When the essays were being returned, I could see the dean at the blackboard, in his black robes, hovering like a bat. His lips quivered. His balding pate seemed to shine with more sweat than was usual and his glasses were all steamed up.

"You." He pointed dramatically at a red-haired boy who sat toward the back of the class.

"Yes, Father." The boy, Liam, stood up.

"Where did you come across this . . . this heresy . . . this . . ."—he spat out the word—"Darwinism."

I could see a smile tugging at the corner of Liam's lips. "In a book, Father."

"And, judging by your precise quotations and by the accurate references in your bibliography, I presume that this offensive text has been sneaked into this hallowed place."

"Not sneaked, Father. Brought."

"Give it to me."

Liam lifted his desk and rustled through textbooks and papers. I just saw the title, *The Origin of Species*, as he put the book into the outstretched hand that was awaiting it. The dean made a great show of ripping the pages from the spine, tearing them across and crumpling them into the wastepaper bin. The smile was gone from Liam's mouth. He looked more like crying as his essay, in the same torn and crumpled state, followed Darwin into the bin.

"In the future, the only books you're allowed to read are those in the seminarians' library." The dean's face was a peculiar shade of purple as he left the classroom.

"But it doesn't make any sense," Liam protested to me later. "The Adam and Eve story is a Creation myth. It's not meant to be enshrined as an irrefutable fact of our existence."

A few days after that, I found a book on evolution among the "permitted" texts in the library. Written by

Père Teilhard de Chardin, it allowed the theory of evolution within a Christian framework. Matter was seen as continually striving toward life, as life strove toward intelligence and intelligence, in turn, aspired to spirituality. The ultimate aim of all evolutionary movement was toward communion with the Divine.

Thrilled with my discovery, I brought the book to Liam and he rewrote his essay to the begrudging satisfaction of the dean.

From then on, Liam and I were inseparable. On walks, or excursions, or during our prayerful striding round the cloister garden, we seemed to always fall into step together. He loved a good argument. And he never gave me the satisfaction of winning. I would no sooner seem to have convinced him of my point of view than he would turn and argue its exact opposite. For Liam, there were always ten different aspects to everything and answers, if there were any, came in twenty shades of monochrome.

He challenged me, frightened me, but drew me like a magnet. The dean wrote to my parents and complained about our closeness.

After the first holidays, Liam came back changed. He seemed to be avoiding me. I couldn't understand it. Then one night late, he called to my room. He sat quiet and morose, on the single chair beside the bed.

"I think I'm going to have to leave," he said eventually.

"But you haven't explained anything."

"I mean the college, the Church."

"Why?"

"Because I'm gay."

He flicked his hair back out of his eyes and tucked it behind one ear. The gesture seemed suddenly and obviously effeminate. I had never thought of him in that context before, but I understood that what he said was true.

I laughed, suddenly, self-consciously but happily, because it didn't seem a legitimate reason for him to leave.

"You haven't done anything sexual, have you?"

He shook his head. "But I've checked all the books in the library. I've read everything they say. And what it boils down to is that being gay is a state of sin in itself, without ever doing anything."

"Look. It's much the same for me." I put my hand on his shoulder, naturally, as I always had. But the contact now seemed loaded, so I withdrew my hand. "If I look lustfully at a woman, then I've already sinned with her in my heart. I have to confess that."

"Yes, but you can be forgiven. I can't. Because I can't reform myself. I can't stop being what I am."

"The state of being human is a state of sinfulness. But as celibate priests, we deny the demands of the flesh and place ourselves on a higher spiritual plane, above other men. Not in a superior or condescending way, but so that we can be worthy to relate to God on man's behalf. You're as worthy as anyone."

"I can't believe that being human is sinful any more

than being gay. Or that anyone is more or less worthy regardless of whether they're celibate. You live in a fantasy world, Ciarán. And you don't let anyone get deep enough to challenge anything you think."

When he was leaving, my instinct was to hug him, to prove him wrong. But I drew back, afraid, ashamed. I never saw him again. For me, it was the closest I ever came to friendship.

Many more succumbed to the lure of the world outside the seminary walls during the year. As each one left, I became more determined to follow through on my vocation. No woman, or creed, or need, would seduce me. What Liam had said about me probably wasn't true when he said it, but it became true. And through the endless battles that I waged against my human, sinful self, the refrain rang warmly in my ears—"And Ciarán spent thirty years in perfection of body and spirit."

Only a handful of us were ordained at the end of seven years, amid gloomy predictions for the future of the priesthood and the Church and rumors that the seminary was to close. It was 1982.

More special for me than my ordination was my first Mass in the cathedral at home. I stood for the first time, dressed in my sacramental robes, facing the people, my back to the tabernacle, and a wild joy engulfed me.

"On the night He was betrayed He took bread, broke it, gave it to his disciples and said: "This is my body that will be given up for you . . ." As I raised the host, I looked up and saw the huge circular window at the back sending swirls of light across the bowed heads of the congregation. "Do this in memory of me. Again He took the cup . . ." I raised the chalice and the gold of it shone in the colored light. "This is the cup of my blood. The blood of the new and everlasting covenant that has been shed for you and for all men so that sins may be forgiven. Do this in memory of me. Lord, I am not worthy to receive you. But only say the word and I shall be healed."

I drank of the chalice of Christ's blood. Through this communion, I was closer than I had ever been to God. I had reached the spiritual pinnacle of my life. Only death, I thought, would bring me closer than this. For the first time in many years, I imagined my brother's angelic face smiling down at me. This moment brought me closer to him, too.

It was two years later that the white pickup van brought me and my few possessions along the road where the dust devils played . . .

I look up and notice that there is a gardener working in the garden. He is brushing the grass with a broom made of sticks, piling up the dead leaves and blossoms into neat piles. I feel the sunshine on my face. I look at the jacaranda blossoms and the flower beds flanking the steps that lead down to the lower garden where he is absorbed, but slow, at his task. It is a tranquil scene, I

reflect. Quiet. Suburban. Safe. Beautiful. The nearest
place there is, maybe, to heaven on earth. These are my
thoughts as I watch the gardener turn and walk up the
steps toward me. He hasn't noticed me. He is still absorbed in his own thoughts, his own task. His head
bobs higher and higher until it's level with mine. We
see each other and stop, dumbstruck, at the recognition. I am looking into the eyes of my killer. He is
looking into the eyes of the dead.

The gardener recovers himself. Moves up the last
step and proceeds toward me, slowly, a little sheepishly,
his hand outstretched.

"Baba Kilani."

I take his hand and feel the soft flesh and calluses
under my fingers.

"Irungu."

Shiku is in the sitting room when I stagger in through
the patio doors.

"Irungu," I tell her. "Irungu is in the garden."

"Yes," she says, "I have given him a job as gardener."

I draw the heavy gates across the patio. Clang them
shut. Snap the padlock closed.

She looks up from the pile of exercise books she is
correcting. There is a red pen in her hand. She is wearing glasses that I haven't seen her wear before. "He called
to the gate, last week, looking for money. How could I
turn him away? He is Wambui's husband."

I slide the glass doors across. Turn the key in the lock.

"Ciarán, what are you doing?"

"Got to lock the doors. All the doors. Irungu is the one. Shiku . . . quick!"

"What?"

I have collapsed into an armchair, shaking, gibbering. "Shiku, the doors . . ." My heart is thundering. I am afraid that I will pass out before I can tell her, warn her.

"Good God!" She jumps up and heads toward the kitchen. There is a clank as she closes the metal gates on the front door. I hear her turning keys in all the outside doors. She returns with a glass of brandy and forces it into my hand. I take it. Sip. Gulp the liquid down. Feel the heat of it hit my stomach.

"He was the one with the *panga*."

"Are you sure?"

"He thought I was dead."

"Everyone thinks you're dead."

"You must call the police."

"Why?"

"That man's a murderer."

"You're alive."

"But Irungu . . ."

"It is okay, Ciarán. Nobody will harm you. The doors are barred. Irungu, just now, is gathering his things to go home—to the shanty where he is living with his second wife and his children."

"What if he brings a gang of men and comes back for me?"

"You're being ridiculous, Ciarán. I will go and speak with Irungu."

"You can't go out there. He'll harm you."

"Irungu?" She laughs. "Irungu won't touch me. We've known each other all our lives."

Shiku opens the patio door, hands me back the keys and clicks the padlock closed again behind her.

"I will return soon, no problem."

My hand trembles as I take the keys and watch her disappear around the corner to the servants' quarters.

I sit back down in the chair and drain the rest of the brandy. The time she is away seems so long. Each jangling second piles on the next. My mind contorts itself into patterns of fear, into a thousand imagined outcomes, all of which involve her death. I see the *panga* rise and fall, hear Shiku scream. There are *panga*s in the servants' quarters. How could I let her go? I should protect her. I should go outside now and fight the man who is strangling her with his bare hands. But I can't move. My legs have changed to quivering jelly.

It is still light when Shiku reappears, smiling, signaling for me to open the doors.

"It is okay; Irungu has gone now. He is very happy to see you alive. He was afraid that your God would send him to hell for what he had done. Now, he has seen a miracle with his own eyes and he will be a good, Christian man. Poor Irungu!"

"*Poor* Irungu?"

"He is already dying, Ciarán. Would you want him to spend the rest of his days in prison?"

I tremble all over now. My body shudders with tension and relief. My teeth chattered uncontrollably. I am frozen with cold. Tears fall. I feel Shiku sit on the arm of my chair. She puts her arms around me, holds me, kisses my hair as a mother would comfort her child. I lean into her for warmth. Nuzzle my face against her neck, taste with my lips the sweet taste of sweat on her skin. "It is okay," she says. "Irungu has no will or no strength to harm you now."

I am diverted, suddenly, from the task that has seemed my only reality. Although I climb the steps and sit before my desk and the blank page, I cannot think about my past. Instead, my thoughts are of Irungu.

What do I know of Irungu? He is a man like any other man. His broad, dashing smile, with me, maybe never quite reached his eyes. But I didn't notice that at the time. And now, maybe I'm reinventing those younger eyes as cold.

His eyes haunt my waking and my sleeping. Always, above them, the *panga* raised, falling, falling, falling, over and over. And always those eyes, filled with hatred. Killer eyes—that I now know to be the eyes of Irungu. The scar, remembered now, twisting through the right eyebrow. I had thought I had seen only the eyes! How memory deludes us. How the subconscious mind censors what it knows and only shows us what we're prepared to see.

I search through the pages of my memoirs. They seem so authoritative in their tone. How much of them is really true? How much is fabrication? How much is delusion? Already, in dragging myself out of the depths of unknowing, I have presumed to know too much.

My doubts add to my nightmares, my fears. I no longer walk outside with Muthoni. No longer eat biscuits with tea on the patio. I eat very little and I grow weak. Nurse Esther scolds constantly. The pages of my life remain unwritten.

During these days, I have become custodian of the keys, carrying the huge rattling bundle with me everywhere. I am like a jailer, locking Shiku and Muthoni and the ayah out, responding to the doorbell and letting them in again. I can see that this paranoia of mine is irritating Shiku. She has been muttering about doubling up on sets of keys.

A sound outside my window draws me to my feet. Irungu is clipping the grass. I notice that his body is turning frail now, the slasher moving rhythmically up and over his shoulder. Slowly round again, *clip whish*, *clip whish* and the streams of sweat coursing down his bony back. I don't see a monster. I see a man. A dying man.

I take my images of Irungu to my pages and I write what I cannot know. I write what, on the surface, appears to be untrue. What can I know of Irungu, after all? How can I begin to understand the reality of another human being? Is this man working in the garden the same man that I write in my story? No. The mind and heart of another cannot be seen by me, or written for that matter. And how can I represent a man from another culture who wears another skin? Yet, by inventing a life for him, a set of events partly based on my interpretation of what has happened, I come closer to finding the man. Sometimes, in this new Irungu who takes shape beneath my pen, I glimpse some aspect of myself and I can try to encapsulate that essential something in my writing, however inadequate that is. On some level, I understand that, in writing this Irungu, I am only delving into hidden parts of myself. My fictions flow on to the page, making more sense of my world than the memoirs ever did.

Tonight, I have asked Shiku if she will listen to my gardener story. So, after the child has gone to bed, she links my arm and brings me down the steps to the sitting room.

"It is nice to have company," she says. "Sitting here alone is no fun."

We sit on opposite chairs. I'm nervous reading this to her, worried about what she'll think of my interpretation of her tribesman, her gardener, her friend. My killer. I hear my own voice reverberating back from the parquet floor, the walls, the windows. Hear it wash around her as she sits so still, so intent. I offer her my story as her daughter offers me flowers. Only more reverently. Because her opinion matters so much.

The story ends. I catch a break in my voice. Clear my throat. Wait. She considers. Then she says: "Who is this strange white woman you have brought to live in my house?"

"She's me. Well, maybe not quite me. Some feminine part of myself. But she doesn't exist outside my head."

"I do not understand why you write lies."

I'm disappointed with this response. I try to justify myself to her. "They're not lies. They're fictions. The truths that they contain are deeper than anything I could say if I were limited to what really happened. How can I know Irungu? What he thinks? What he feels?"

"I understand, Ciarán." She leans across to touch my hand, to quell my need to explain, to reassure me. "This is not Irungu as I know him. In parts, yes, maybe. But how well can I know him, either? Even I, if I tried to write about my own husband, could not know him well enough to write a true picture. How can we know anyone like that?"

"The reason I have to write this is so I can understand why he did what he did to me. Why he hates me as he does."

"Irungu has his own complex reasons for the things he does. The woman in this story is a stranger—an innocent newcomer. Maybe you should put yourself in this story. See if, in some way, you are responsible for Irungu's anger."

"Now you're blaming me."

"No," she says gently, leaning toward me, catching my hand in hers. Her dark eyes look warmly into mine. "I am trying to see all sides. Maybe you should try writing it from Irungu's perspective."

There is no point in arguing with her. But I am not ready to believe what she says. I move away from her and she settles herself back on her chair. A whiff of her perfume reaches me. She smells of flowers.

12

Our conversations have been shallow since her birthday. We sidestep matters of the heart and feelings. She avoids touching me or sitting too close. Julius has become a regular topic in her musings. Although I resent his intrusion into our time together, these hours after sunset become my favorites. I read while she is busy with her copy books. Occasionally, we watch a film on television.

Still, I observe Irungu, seeing his slow trail around the gardens. Sometimes I watch him double over in a coughing fit, his hands clutching his stomach as he gasps for breath. Shiku is right, I am beginning to see. This man's anger has been spent and he is no threat to me.

So I begin to leave the doors unlocked during the daytime, when Shiku isn't here. And Irungu goes about his gardening, oblivious to whether they are open or closed. I relinquish the keys.

I chance a walk with Muthoni. As soon as we appear at the patio, the gardener hastens his steps toward the rabbit hutch and releases Sungura to join us. We proceed through the yard of the servants' quarters where the clothes are steaming dry on the clothesline and we reach the front garden with its high wall and big double gates. Along the front wall there is a mass of multicolored bougainvillea bushes, their twisted tendrils and their thorns weaving in and out of a bed of barbed wire. A trap for any unsuspecting thief who might attempt to jump over the wall. I look back at the house, the ornate wrought-ironwork making black cages over the windows. Black wrought-iron screens over the doors, open now, during the daytime. A pretty feature, almost, these necessities of security. The orange terra-cotta tiles are built over an impenetrable concrete roof. All these things designed to keep the enemy out. But what if the enemy is locked inside with you? Despite the "protection" of the child, I feel uneasy.

Above the gates there is a Nandi flame tree covered in giant, tulip-shaped flowers. As we watch, they drift down onto the macadam. Muthoni gives a shriek of delight and runs forward to catch them during their slow descent. As she runs, the rabbit bounds in front of her. She stumbles. Falls. She and the rabbit are lying in a heap on the ground. I try to go to her aid. But Irungu is there before me. I had not noticed him watching us.

"Don't touch her," I want to shout. But I see him smile, bend on one knee, lift the child up and dust her off. She puts her arm around his neck.

"Are you hurt, little one?" he asks tenderly. She lifts her knee to him for inspection. Her face is sad.

"It is not broken," he says. "There is no blood. It will be okay, little one."

He touches the knee gently. Hugs the child to him. She smiles, then laughs and runs again to gather the fallen blossoms.

I look across to where Irungu is standing. Of course, in this culture, children are revered. Even the most hardened criminal would not harm a child. Besides, Irungu is a family man. I remember his dead daughter.

Still, I look edgily at Irungu. He keeps his eyes averted. He will not look straight into my eyes. Downcast, clouded windows hide a warring soul. I remember them full of hatred. I remember them cold. I cannot look at them now. I turn away.

We watch the little girl as she scoops up the huge, orange flowers, each one bigger than her hand. She hangs flowers on the rabbit's ears. The long ears twitch and the petals scatter. Sungura nibbles at them.

"Silly rabbit." Muthoni laughs. "Don't eat the flowers!" She rolls on the ground with the rabbit and the fallen petals.

When she looks up and sees me standing unsupported, she remembers her duties. She rushes to pick some sprigs from a bush and brings them to me. Remembers Irungu. Runs and gathers more for him.

"Smell!" she says, dangling the bunch under my nose. The scent is sweet and heady.

The flowers are unusual. They are in sets of threes, one mauve, one white, and the third a mixture of both colors.

"Do they have a name?" I ask.

"Some funny name," Muthoni says.

"Yes," says Irungu. "They are called yesterday, today, and tomorrow."

"They're about hope, then," I find myself saying.

Irungu's eyes meet mine for a flickering second before we each remember that tomorrow has shut down. And I remember that he is the one to blame. Yet in that glance there is something of a recognition of each other, a sense of our common fate. If I could forgive him, I could almost pity him. Pity? What am I talking about?

I try to recall everything that I have ever heard or known about Irungu. In my delving, I find that I know his wife, Wambui, better than I know him. So, this time, in my writing I begin with her.

Shiku goes silent when I read her this story. There are tears in her eyes.

"Wambui," she says. "She always seemed more solid than the rest of us. Her life was mapped out, as mine never could be. She would marry Irungu and live her days in Kishagi. She would bear children who would care for her into old age. You are right. Her only ambition was to have a stone house like my mother's."

"And a monogamous marriage."

"Why do you want to blame Irungu for everything? Don't you see he is a victim, too?"

I am unable to answer her.

"What do you expect Irungu to do? To live alone in the city?"

"You do it."

"That is not the same."

"It's different for a woman, you mean?"

"Yes," she says in a self-satisfied way.

"I have never, ever, been with a woman."

Shiku laughs suddenly. "Do you know what Irungu used to say about you?"

"What did he say?" I ask, angrily.

Shiku pauses, regretting what she has begun to say.

"What did he say about me?" I quiet my voice, anxious to know.

"He said you were a eunuch." She flushes at her own directness and tries to backtrack. "It was part of a theme of his about priests. That if they wanted Christians they should beget them instead of encouraging the young men of the tribe to become celibate, like them. Irungu never liked priests—any priest. It was not you particularly."

"A eunuch," I say bitterly. "Well, thanks to him, I am now."

"He didn't . . .?"

I shake my head. "But he might as well have for all

the response . . ." Good God, what am I talking to this woman about? I falter. Close my eyes.

She is sitting on the couch beside a stack of copy books. Her reading glasses make her look studious and oddly European. All day I have been distracted by thoughts of her. I have been hounded by unbearable longing. This isn't lust, I tell myself, this is love. I cannot bear to be so near and yet so distant from her.

There is a small space left on the couch. I squeeze in beside her. My eyes are on the buttons of her blouse. There's a notion in my head that if I can release the smell of her, it will satiate my need.

I touch the cloth of her blouse where it is stretched taut across her breast. Feel the hard disc of a button. My hand shakes as I fumble with it. The buttonhole is too small. I see tiny stitches on either side of the hole. The button is held in place, tightly. She seems intent on her work. If only I can open that button without her noticing, perhaps she will not reject me. Why should I think that? Why should I expect a response from her? A married woman blessed by my own blessing. And I a . . . no, not even a priest anymore. Just a lost soul. This is all there has ever been. This longing. Call it by its name— this lusting. This futility.

As I move to withdraw my hand, I feel my fingers held. I look into her face. Her eyes are hidden by the glasses. She is, seemingly, uninterested and she doesn't appear to notice what I have tried to do. There is no sign of desire in her face, yet my fingers are held in hers. The button budges and opens. My trembling fingers, guided by hers, open button after button until those dark breasts lie exposed. Vulnerable. Irresistible. I bury my face in their scented skin. It seems as if her heart is thundering as loudly as my own.

Shiku raises my head and looks solemnly into my eyes. She has removed her glasses. What I read in those eyes is not lust, but pain. "Ciarán, if you try to seduce me, I do not know that I can resist."

"Shiku, ah, my love."

She will deny me nothing now. Hope, joy, anticipation, and desire clamor for the highest place. I lift up the teacher-ish skirt, find the smooth curve of her thighs. She takes my hand gently in hers. Not here, she motions. "Shhh!" She leads me to my bedroom where she locks the door behind us.

Shiku's flowery perfume suffuses the air as she loosens and removes her clothes. I can barely breathe. Deftly, she undresses me, pausing to give a little gasp as she sees my scars, not so livid now, but still prominent. She kisses them, then continues with her undressing. Gives a little laugh. "Ah," she says, "it seems that Irungu has not done you so much damage!" She leads me to the bed. Teaches me. I lose myself in her. She brings me over the threshold. I am falling, falling. I am dying again. Only this time, I am not alone. I am wrapped in the embrace of my beloved. And this time I am not cast out to purgatory, but lie back in the crook of my lover's arm.

"Now you are a man," she says triumphantly, lying back against the pillows, watching the gecko.

"You make me more than a man," I answer. And I notice the figures in the batik on the wall: the two heads together, kissing, the pot that they carry, the communal womb, the funnel. I have joined the ranks of the initiated. Everything is clear and tinged with joy.

"I love you, Shiku."

Shiku flicks off the light and black velvet darkness envelops us. I am safe in her arms. Sungura scrabbles outside the window.

When I awake, at dawn, she is still beside me. I pull back the curtains, pull back the sheet and let the daylight flood over her body.

Reverently, I touch those voluptuous breasts, kiss those large, curving hips, run my finger, wonderingly, into the small depression of her navel. Her eyelids flicker and she eyes me sleepily, watching me watching her, a playful smile on her lips. She giggles, girlishly, as I continue my exploration into the secret places that have known me, but that I do not yet know intimately. I am relieved to find that her clitoris is intact. At least, Christianity has spared her that ritual mutilation.

"Don't touch me there. It is a sin."

"There is no sin anymore."

No, this is not a sin. This is an act of worship. I am kneeling at the shrine of a woman's loveliness. I am humbled and prostrate before her. The biblical term offers itself to me—to *know* a woman. I am knowing my beloved Shiku.

When she has been satisfied, she lies listless and exhausted in my arms. "I never knew that it could feel like this. How did you know?"

"It just made sense to me that the removal of the clitoris must have something to do with reducing pleasure, so that a woman would remain faithful and submissive."

"We thought it was all about growing up."

"And I thought celibacy was about denial of the flesh."

"Is it not?"

"It's about denial of the spirit. Denial of love. It rivals religious experience. That's why it was banned. I understand, now, that this was what my father wanted for me in my life. He couldn't bear to see me celibate."

"He would not approve of me."

"Why wouldn't he?"

"Because I am a black, African woman."

I think about my father. Consider for a while. "No. He would have disapproved of you because you're married."

***

Today, I don't feel afraid anymore. I take my notebook and pen and I face, brazenly, out to the garden. There is a wooden deckchair under a jacaranda. I start to drag the chair out beyond the shade of the trees.

In a second, Irungu is there.

"No, Fatha. This one is too heavy. You must not."

He pulls the chair. It is too heavy for him. We lift it together, place it in the sun. Two wrecks of men. We think the same thought, maybe. He flashes his brilliant smile and his eyes light for a moment, until he remembers and the blinds come down again.

As I write in my notebook, I feel Irungu's eyes on me all the time. It makes me uneasy. What is he thinking, now? I wonder. The old dread stifles me as I see him turn, suddenly, decisively, at the bottom of the garden and walk quickly up the steps, straight toward me.

Irungu goes on his knees at my feet. He dips his finger in the dust and makes the sign of the cross and then, with dust, repeats the cruciform shape on his forehead and chest.

"Forgive me, Baba Kilani."

I look down at the thick mat of his hair, silvering already round the edges.

"I forgive you."

"No. You must say the proper words."

I lay my hands on Irungu's head. "I . . . no longer have the power . . ."

I have worshipped at the shrine of a woman's nakedness. I am no longer a priest. There is no God. How can I tell Irungu this?

He looks up at me with tears in his eyes. "Please, Baba Kilani."

I say some Latin words. Something approximating the words of forgiveness. I cannot bring myself to blaspheme like this. My spiritual integrity is in tatters. "Go now, my son, and sin no more."

Irungu kisses my hand and rises to his feet, his eyes glistening with happiness and unshed tears. "Thank you, Baba Kilani." He raises his eyes to the sky. "Thank you, Ngai."

My days are filled with the fascination of another human being. Her heart, her mind, her body, her soul, her words, her thoughts, her needs, her dreams. I cannot drink in enough of her.

Once, after love, I call her "goddess."

"Don't call me that," she says. "I am a human woman, nothing more. If you put me up too high, there is nothing I can do but fall down. Then you will not respect me. You will blame me for having fallen."

"No place is too high for you, my love, my angel."

"Did you ever hear about the old *matumba*?"

"The old bus?"

"Yes, when a woman gets too old she is traded in, like an old bus, and replaced by a newer model."

"This is propaganda, to keep you humble."
"Is it less real than goddesses and angels?"

Our todays become yesterdays and gather behind us. We celebrate a month of love. And then another. Shiku is thirty years, three months and one week old. I am five months old by my new reckoning. Forty-two years and ten months by the old. The face in the glass has become my own again. There is a light in the eyes and a healthiness in the cheeks that I do not want to see. I want to stay locked in here in this endless day of love.

The question of a future comes into sharp focus with the advent of an unwanted guest. Shiku knocks at my door loudly and there is an anxious edge on her voice. "Father Ciarán," she calls, "Father Madden is here to see you."

Madden has no patience with these pleasantries. He barges straight in. I am dressed and sitting at my desk, but the bed is unmade after the night's passions. And the smell of her perfume is strong in the air.

He sniffs and sits down. Shiku tries to pull the bed-clothes into shape. "This house girl!" she exclaims. "She never comes to work on time." I catch Shiku's eye and the wicked wink and grin behind Madden's back. In spite of my efforts to control them, my lips twitch into a smirk. She manages to turn a giggle into a "Hrrump" of disgust. "Staff these days!" Shiku bolts for the door.

I know that, once outside, she'll laugh herself silly over this pathetic little man for whom we perform these lies.

"Interesting batik," he says, "what is it?"

"Oh, it's just an abstract."

"Isn't that a pot?"

"Oh, maybe you're right. I hadn't noticed that." I'm tempted to tell him it is a test of manhood.

"Still in pain?" he asks at my excruciated expression.

"My stitches," I gasp.

"The doctor says you're ready to return to Ireland. I've booked you on a flight for next Tuesday."

"I'm not going."

"Let me remind you, Keerin, of your vow of obedience. The bishop has already tolerated more than enough of your insubordination."

His eyes roam over the room. I notice them pausing on the bed. I look to see if there is any evidence left behind. A stain? Forgotten underwear? An earring? Every time he looks toward the bed I have a vision of Shiku lying there naked, her beautiful brown body opening to receive me. And I keep thinking that he is seeing the same thing or sensing it. All that Catholic guilt mounts up in me, making my blood pound in my poor damaged veins. It threatens to suffocate me. And this self-righteous little bigot sits there judging me. He seems to say *I can read your mind. I could have told you years ago you were a sinner.* There is no defense that I can offer. I am morally compromised.

"It has come to the attention of the bishop . . ."

He pauses.

It has come to the attention of the bishop that you are screwing this woman.

Yes, they are the kind of words he would use—screw, fuck, fornicate. Words that debase. As if that were what Shiku and I do together.

No, Father. Actually, it was more sacramental than that—like a communion of hearts, bodies, spirits all together. Love, Father.

But he is not talking about that at all. He is waffling on about politics and political involvement and the priestly mission to guide beyond the temporal to the eternal. It strikes me suddenly that he doesn't know. Can't know. And could never even suspect because, in his blinkered, twisted thinking, he could never conceive the thought that I might stoop so low as to do it with a black woman. In a stark moment of realization I encounter a new emotion—hatred for this hypocrite. It is the direct opposite of the profound and sacred feeling that Shiku evokes in me. At last, I rise above him, morally superior.

"His Grace has asked me to tell you that you won't be returning to Kishagi."

"You mean I'm dismissed?"

"It's for your own protection. And it's best that you return to Ireland immediately."

"I'm in no danger. The attack was personal, not political."

"Oh?" He raises his eyebrows. "Do you know something the police don't?"

"I know nothing. Outside the confessional."

"I see." Although his hair is white, there are black whiskers poking out of his nose.

"Tell the bishop I refuse to leave. And that I'll speak with him personally when I'm ready."

"You can't do that!"

"If he doesn't take that, you can tell him to stick his bishopric up his arse."

Father Madden scuttles to his feet, sidles to the door like a cockroach fleeing before a hobnailed boot. "You'll regret this you little . . ."

"Little what, Father?"

But he doesn't wait to explain. What was it he was going to call me? A pup? A little pup? That phrase from childhood. I grin to myself.

When I recount the story to Shiku, her reaction is not the laugh that I expect. She looks shocked. "What are you going to do?"

"Live by my own rules with my own sweet angel and never think about tomorrow." I am still high from the encounter with Madden.

"You cannot live on my husband's charity."

"Let's escape. We'll run away together like a pair of teenagers."

"On what?"

She turns and walks away from me.

Suddenly, I see the enormity of what I have done. Outside of the Church, I have nothing. No home, no profession, no job, no car, not even the price of airfare back to Ireland or a taxi to Kishagi. All I own in this world is a beat-up stereo and a collection of dog-eared secondhand books.

Perhaps it is my anxiety that mars our evenings, but talk diminishes. The television fills in for us. Or books, which we read side by side on the sofa. And the nights' lovemaking is cooler, less intense, more distant. But maybe that is my imagination.

We are awakened by a cry in the night. Immediately, Shiku switches on the light and runs from the room.

"Mommy, Mommy." I hear the terror in the child's voice. "Where were you?"

"Ciarán called me to bring him a cup of tea." I am sure that even a child could see through the lie. Her mother is wrapped in, but not quite wearing, a dressing gown. There was no light visible under my door. I lay my head back on the pillow and groan. How long have we feared and expected this discovery of our secret?

But Muthoni's crying hasn't stopped. She needs more than the comfort of her mother's presence. Shiku appears briefly in the doorway, the child bundled in her arms. "She's burning with fever." I can see the little girl's eyes, bright and glassy. She is too ill to even notice the circumstances in which she has found us. The first anxiety seems small in comparison to the worry that follows it.

"Okay, baby, okay," Shiku soothes her as she carries the child to her room. Used as I am to sick calls in the night, I am already dressed and padding barefoot at her heels. She strips the clothes from the still made-up bed in her own bedroom and lays Muthoni on the sheet, one hand anxiously feeling her forehead. "Calpol. Kitchen. Second cupboard on the right," she orders and I obey.

Muthoni cannot keep the medicine down. Shiku goes to the bathroom for a basin of water and a towel. The child shivers and cries as her body is sponged with the cold water. I stay with them for what seems a long time, watching the intense love with which Shiku handles her daughter. The constant stroking of her hands. The smoothing back of the tousled hair, which is sticking to Muthoni's forehead with sweat.

As I look around this room into which I have never been invited before, I notice the oversized slippers at the foot of the bed, the ashtray on the locker. I think of the absent father. Think of the incongruity of my presence here. I catch myself wishing to fit those slippers, to fit that role. Of all the gaps that have opened in my life, this is the one that aches most. My celibacy has denied me ordinary family relationships: father and child, child and father, husband and wife, mother and child—the whole domestic scene in which my own father reveled.

Shiku is exhausted. I take over the toweling, rinsing out the cloth and wiping and cooling the hot, fevered skin of the child's face and neck and chest. At last, her eyes droop. Her thumb finds its way into her mouth. She sleeps. Shiku checks her forehead and smiles. "We are winning."

"Thank God." My answer, although it may be addressed to no one, is a genuine prayer of thanks.

Muthoni's illness, alarming though it seemed, is no more than tonsillitis. The doctor orders a few days rest and a prescription for antibiotics. At night, Shiku stays with her in the big double bed. I sit with her during the day and read her stories. The ayah is grateful for my help. She is used to her own routine during the hours when Muthoni is usually in school.

The child and I are reading a favorite *sungura* story, when the telephone rings. She picks up the extension telephone on the bedside locker beside her mother's bed.

"Hello. Yes. Good. Very good. When? No, Mommy is not here. I am sick in bed. Bwana Ciarán is with me."

She hands me the telephone. "My Daddy wants to talk to you."

"Bwana Ciarán." The voice on the line is audibly sarcastic, even at this distance.

"It's . . . it's Muthoni's name for me. She has tonsillitis. I'm looking after her." I am imagining how Julius must picture this scene, what he's thinking about finding me in his bedroom. With his daughter. No doubt he has heard of all the defilement done by priests. I decide that I don't care what he thinks. It is unworthy.

"I thought you were recovered. I thought you were gone. My wife hasn't mentioned you for ages."

"I am recovered, yes. Can I give Shiku a message?"

"Ask Wanjiku to ring me." He doesn't waste any time over pleasantries.

Muthoni takes the receiver from me and puts it back on the cradle. "My daddy is coming home," she announces happily.

13

Shiku appears from her bedroom and her scent is strong. She is wearing the birthday dress—the green one with the pink and purple flowers.

"Where are you going?"

"I am going out."

"Where? With whom?"

"Why should I tell you? Even my husband does not try to own me as you do."

I catch her by the sleeve of her dress, try to hold her. As she pulls away there is the sound of ripping cloth. In her eyes, I see tears of defiance. Or sadness. Maybe even fear.

"I cannot stay locked up in this house with you. I will go mad. And anyway, people will be suspicious."

I let her go. All night, I pace the sitting room floor, waiting, wondering, worrying. Loving her, hating myself.

It is after three o'clock when she returns.

"I am sorry," she says, "but it frightens me that you are making your whole life around me. How can I be that much to you? To anyone?"

"I am sorry, too."

"You cannot stay hiding here forever. It is months since you were outside these gates. You do nothing; you don't even write anymore."

She hasn't mentioned the homecoming. It is I who ask: "What will he do if he finds out?"

"He will probably beat me."

"I won't let him touch you."

"You will have no say in it," she says, almost smugly. "At least if he beats me I know where I am with him. That he wants me. That he will take me back."

"And you would go back to him? On those terms?"

She nods her head slowly. "I do not fear my husband's fists as much as I fear your obsessive love."

The wrought-iron gates of the massive front door are unlocked and sprawled open. Muthoni is dressed up in a frilly frock and all afternoon she has been skipping up to the hall every time a sound comes from the street outside. She is irritating me with her skittishness. I close the book that I have been reading to her.

"The story is not yet finished," she says.

"It is. You weren't listening."

"Are you annoyed because my daddy is coming back?"

"No!" I force a smile on my face. "Of course I'll be very happy to see Julius. I missed him."

"I missed him, too."

A car door bangs and the child runs to the door.

The big man enters, drops his suitcases on the floor and lifts his daughter up in a great hug. She shrieks with happiness.

"Ah, look at you, how you've grown, little one." He shifts her to one hip and carries her effortlessly down the steps and throws open the patio doors. He sniffs the air and breathes it in deeply, then turns to greet me, where I am sitting.

"You are much recovered, Baba," he says, smiling.

Shiku follows behind him, smiling too, talking excitedly. She seems to share the enthusiasm of this reunion. She is light-stepped, bubbly, joyous even, in his company. I look for some trace of insincerity in her demeanor, but there is none that I can detect. Either she is a great actress, or she is genuinely thrilled to see him home.

I am suddenly out of place here among this family, so I escape to the garden where Irungu is unhitching a goat that since yesterday has been tethered to the fence; its plaintive bleating kept me awake all night. Now I watch as Irungu takes a sharp knife and slits the animal's throat. The cut is as accurate as any surgeon's incision. Irungu knows what he is doing. The only cries are the cries of fear that precede the slaughter. They cease at once. There is no pain. The death is instant, humane. These judders and kicks are not death throes but the muscular spasms of the already dead. As if the body is caught, unaware of its own demise, in the same

way that a chicken will continue running around the
yard, following posthumously the directions of its sev-
ered head.

Irungu holds the goat firmly and lets the blood flow
out into a basin. Hardly a drop has been spilt on the
coarse brown-and-white fur.

"Are you squeamish, Baba Kilani?"

I look him directly in the eye and shake my head.
No, I am not squeamish. I am thinking of the birds and
animals that Irungu carves out of sticks and pieces of
wood. Thinking of his skill with knives.

"Why did you use a *panga*?"

He looks up, not understanding for a second. Can
he have forgotten so soon? A chuckle escapes from
him as he stoops again over his work. "You say the words
of forgiveness and still you do not forgive."

It is true, but I won't allow him the truth of it. "I
have forgiven you. But I'm curious."

"Can you hold this animal over the basin for me?"
he asks. "I am not as strong as I was."

"AIDS."

"Yes."

I swap places with him on the stool. He takes off his
overalls and drapes them over my front to protect my
clothes. Then I take the goat in my lap while Irungu
bends over it and skillfully peels off the skin. The trickle
of blood eases and becomes a gentle dripping into the
basin.

Does he glance at me differently as he plunges the knife in near the throat and runs it swiftly down from neck to anus? Or is that my imagination? It is a female goat, I notice, almost irrelevantly. Irungu carefully removes the entrails. I hold my breath against the stench.

Some of the most prized and tastiest meats are in the abdomen of the goat. These will be cooked first. Already, I can smell the smoke of the fire. Julius is crouched over the grill, blowing the coals to life.

He strides over to where we are and gathers the sweetmeats in a dish. "Ah, Ciarán, I see you are making yourself useful." There is sarcasm in the tone. But I hear Shiku's precise pronunciation of my name in his mouth. He has never spoken my name like that before.

Irungu is leaning over the goat, carving the flesh. His face is close beside mine. He speaks quietly as if speaking to himself.

"We were okay," he says, "until the white man came. He unsettled us first with his religion, telling us that what we believed was primitive and wrong. That there were everlasting flames that would burn us if we did not give up what we believed and believe in his god, instead. Then when we were divided among ourselves, he came and took our land." There is no menace in Irungu's voice. Only sadness. "He turned our society upside down. Left us struggling and homeless in our own land. Seduced our women. Told them they must be monogamous and, at the same time, taught them to be unfaithful. Taught us to read and write and to do mathematics, but left us with menial jobs."

"That was a long time ago, Irungu. I cannot be held responsible—"

"It still goes on, but they call it by a different name. They call it international debt. They pretend it is respectable and say that colonialism is finished, but it is not. And when we got too numerous and too strong, they were afraid and so they gave us AIDS, to destroy us."

"No, Irungu, you're wrong."

He stabs at the flesh of the goat, forcing the blade around a knuckle of bone. For an instant his eyes are as I remembered them. Uncannily the same. I quake. He senses it. Relaxes the eyes with a smile that reaches the mouth as a boyish grin. "It is good for you that I did not think to use a knife."

"If you had, I would be happier than I am now."

"Next time," he says gently, and laughs. His free hand, bloodstained, touches my shoulder in a gesture of comfort. "It is all right, Baba Kilani."

The patio table has been set with four places and two extra chairs have been brought outside. Electric lights have been switched on and three mugs of beer set out on the low table. I note, smugly, the absence of candles and red wine.

"Father Ciarán." Julius invites me with a gesture and a half bow. I take my place beside Muthoni, who is being allowed to stay up late for this occasion. The smoky smell of charcoal and roasting goat has whetted an appetite that I had not expected to find. Julius goes to and fro to the barbecue, dishing up the succulent meat on to a central tray. We wash our hands and eat with our fingers in the traditional way, dipping first into the meat, then into the white, maize-meal porridge on our plates.

After the meal, Muthoni kisses us all goodnight and Shiku goes to tuck her into bed. I am about to excuse myself to go to my room, when Julius comes back from the kitchen with more bottles of beer and insists that I drink some.

Shiku returns and takes her place beside him on the narrow seat. She might have taken Muthoni's vacant chair I think, peevishly. Julius puts a possessive arm around her and massages her neck as he speaks.

"Look," he says, dreamily. "Look at my wife's lovely, graceful neck. It seems so fragile, doesn't it? The first time I saw this remarkable woman, she was drawing water from a well. There were three or four girls there, each more beautiful than the other. But this one, this Wanjiku, lifted up her bucket expertly and poised it perfectly on her head. As she walked, almost danced away, I watched the sunlight playing on the water and the surface was steady as if made of ice, not liquid. Not a drop slopped out. All the other girls slipped and dripped, but not this one. And I knew, then, that I had to have her for my own."

Shiku giggles and pushes at him, playfully. I notice the way her hands, perhaps unconsciously, touch him as she moves and speaks. My heart is tortured by these touches, but there is a fascination, too. I think of the moth being lured by the candle.

"Do not believe what he tells you, Ciarán. We were students together at the university. This man bowled me over with all his sweet talk. Just like, I am sure, he bowled over that woman from the well." She looks up mischievously into his eyes and prods him in the chest, laughing. He doesn't laugh, but knits his brows together, concentrating on his own topic.

"But will she teach my daughter to carry buckets on her head? No. She'll teach her French and English and arithmetic. How many generations does it take to lose that ability? Only one? If you were to put a bucket of water, that full, on the head of a European, her neck would snap. 'Crack,' just like that."

"And why," I ask, "doesn't the tradition get passed down through the male line?"

Julius throws back his head and laughs. "And why, Father Ciarán, doesn't your Church allow women priests?"

Shiku tries to rescue me. "Kikuyu women don't carry things on their heads, Julius. It was a Maasai woman you saw when you visited your mother's people."

Julius ignores her intrusion. "The ability to carry things on one's head is getting lost. How quickly we are losing our native skills and becoming Europeanized, instead of preserving our unique, racial advantages."

Shiku throws me a sympathetic look. This is obviously one of her husband's favorite themes. But still her restless hands stroke and touch him as he speaks. I catch a whiff of her perfume.

"You see an African mother with a young child?" he asks. "She can take her child from her back and place it by her side, beside a fast-moving highway. It will not move, but will, instinctively, cling to its mother. It will not run into the road. Now, take a white woman with her child. If she lets the child free, it will immediately run off, unaware of any danger. It will run right out on the highway. There is a basic survival instinct here that has been lost by Europeans."

I make some excuses about needing sleep.

"You have tired Ciarán out with all your talking," Shiku scolds.

Julius grunts a goodnight. He looks disappointed that he has failed to raise an argument from me.

A while later, I go to the kitchen for a glass of water and I see them, still on the patio, locked together in an embrace.

My sleep is fitful. Wakeful times are tormented with visions of Julius' hands on her body. I see her responding to his touch as she has to mine. These imagined scenes go on and on without relief. The lovers on the wall goad me with their sexual images. The womb, the funnel, the calabash, the pot. I try to concentrate on the pot. The thing that they carry between them. "I suppose you would call it love," she said. If it were just love it would be easier to deal with than these images of the flesh. But even the pot on the lovers' heads cannot hold its integrity. The picture changes and the pot becomes the bucket that Julius admired so much on her head. I see the woman in the batik, laughing, dancing, not spilling a drop and I feel his admiration, his lust, his need to own her. His filthy desires. I cannot allow his feelings the benefit of love. Whatever it is that he shares with Shiku, it cannot be the sacred thing that she and I have carried together.

I drift into sleep and into nightmare. Father Madden lies in the bed beside me and his voice is sonorous and repetitive. *Remember the primary school in Barawana*, he says. He clings to me with cold hands. I realize that he is dead and that it is his corpse that is dragging me down and down with him into the bed. His eyes are terrified and it is my own terror that is reflected in their dead depths. Every time I drift into sleep, he wakes me again with his clinging and his insistence that I listen to his story—that I remember the primary school in Barawana.

I distract myself with thoughts of Irungu. He, who was my greatest threat, becomes my refuge. In the middle of the night, I go to my desk and I write an extension of my gardener story. It is a fiction that goes deeper than any facts I can know for sure. Beneath the differences of him and me, of black and white, of African and Irish, of murderer and murdered, I understand some truth that is common to both of us. I encounter myself, anew, through the eyes of Irungu and acknowledge my own part in provoking his attack. Forgiveness happens on the page.

My writing becomes an excuse to stay in my room and avoid being with my hosts when they are together. Shiku leaves plates of food out for me to heat in the microwave oven. I suspect she is relieved at my absence from the dinner table.

When I am not writing, I spend time in the garden with Irungu. He tells me that he never intended to get involved in a second marriage. At first, it was just the need for sex. Then Maria became the one most often, and most readily, available. So they drifted into a habit of being together. Even then, he would not have thought of setting it up as anything more than a casual thing. But Maria started talking about love, about needs, putting demands on him. He still loved Wambui and had never really thought of loving anyone else. But the city was lonely on his own. The relationship with Maria was convenient. And when he was challenged by Wambui and the whole notion of Christian marriage, he justified it by reverting to his right to be polygamous—a right protected by the customary law.

From my own insights, I understand Wambui's jealousy, but at least she is loved. Hers is a noble role, one that I might even covet for myself, if only Shiku would reassure me of her love.

"Ciarán."

She is here. Standing at my bedroom door, distractedly picking at the sleeve of her blouse. Eyes downcast, as if some speck of dust on the floor has riveted her attention.

"Yes, Shiku, love?"

"What are you going to do, Ciarán? Where are you going to go?" For "where" I interpret "when." I have no doubt that Julius is behind this inquisition.

"I told you," I say with an attempt at flippancy, "there's nothing, only this moment."

"You are sounding too much like an African."

"And why wouldn't I? Isn't my heart the same color as theirs? As yours?"

"It is because they are poor that they cannot afford to think about tomorrow."

"Yeah? Well, I'm poor. I've taken a vow of poverty."

"You have also taken a vow of chastity." I may have prompted and deserved this response, but I never expected Shiku to speak those words and so sharply.

"He's getting to you, Shiku, isn't he? You're changing. Being turned against me."

"I am not changing. I just never was what you made me out to be. All that goodness and light. That is not me. I am a married woman who has been cheating on her husband."

I go to her, try to put my arms around her. She resists me. Steps backward away from me.

"Shiku, don't put yourself down, don't negate our love."

"Love? That was not about love. It was about repayment of a debt! About . . . pity!" Her voice has become so loud and shrill that I am afraid she will alert her husband.

"Shiku, shush!"

"Don't you tell me to shush. Who do you think you are? Why don't you go outside those damn gates? Get out and find some life for yourself outside of me. You do not belong here."

For a while longer, I try to hide away in my room with my pages. Pictures of Shiku flow out of me and into words. I see her picking up my papers in the house in Kishagi after I was attacked. Seek consolation in her grief. Try to tell myself that, really, she loves me, but has been temporarily diverted by her husband.

Then I recall that incident with Shiku in her teens, the event that led me to send her away to boarding school. The story, at first, brings consolation. What was it that she said? "I loved you when I was so young." Wasn't that it?

I come to see it as one of the pivotal events of my life. The moment of lost opportunity. At the time, I had no idea that the incident with Shiku was of any great significance. I fancied her always. Fancied many women. I'm a man after all. Celibacy, if anything, increases that, because it never gets expressed or used up. That sexual drive. That curiosity. That film reel that starts up in your head that you never allow to play through for fear of the beast in yourself, the sinful part that will tie down and enslave the spirit. How strange it was to me when the opposite happened. When, with her, the act of sex, instead of enslavement, brought liberation. Instead of a physical, down-in-the-boots down-in-the-muck-and-dirt experience, it was a spiritual one. I perceived Shiku as the angel who brought me this. Did I really put her on a pedestal high above humanity? Did my love demand something that no human being could give? Did I make her into a goddess? A God substitute, almost. Filling a spiritual niche. Is she right, then, in rejecting me? Can this great love of mine be just an illusion, as transitory and empty as my experience of God and religion?

At last, I am ready to write about my death. It is not fiction, it is truth, as best I can represent it. I put it down on the page as honestly and as accurately as I can. It is surprising that the piece, when it is finished, is so short. The largest moment of my life, one that seemed to take forever to happen and that brought me into eternity and back, can all be written in the space of a few pages.

I look at the face in the mirror, drawn and hollowed around the eyes, but undeniably healthy. What I want to see there is the death's head. My hand, wonderingly, touches the glass of the mirror. It feels cold and smooth. Like marble. I think of birth and death. Between the cold and cold is warmth. This life that flickers in us for a while. If only I had taken that long-lost opportunity with Shiku. If only Irungu had used a knife. If only the doctor had not played god. If only I had the courage to end it.

A remembered smell comes to my nostrils, a scent from childhood and the cathedral at home. The sweet, musky smell of molten wax when the flame has just been snuffed out. I realize that my task is finished. I have written all there is to write about my life.

I go outside to the garden and around to the front. Muthoni and Sungura no longer accompany me. No doubt Muthoni's father has warned her against being too free with me. And Sungura has been confined to his hutch since he attracted the attentions of a predatory kite.

Standing beneath the Nandi flame tree, I watch the petals drift down. "Go outside those damn gates," she said. I look at them: big, black, iron gates. There is nothing remarkable about them apart from their solidity, their strength, their effectiveness in keeping people out. Or in. Even if I wanted to, I could not go outside without calling Irungu to bring a key for the padlock. Of course if I really wanted to, I could arrange to leave. But these gates have acquired a significance, a symbolism, that is known only to me. They are the gates to my future. And on some level I am afraid that if I pass through them I will find that there is nothing there. The future has shut down on me and locked me in. I am petrified with fear. Unable to take that step.

There is a commotion in the shrubbery. "Tss tss" the sound goes. "Tss tss tss." I listen to it for a while, not taking any real notice. Until I hear a squeal, a shriek of pain. I turn and make my way slowly to a shrub that is bright with blossoms. Two sun birds are fighting. I know these little birds well. Often, in the mornings, I see one of them attacking its reflection in my window.

But today the quarry is real. And the fight is vicious. These beautiful birds are locked together in mortal combat. I wish I had a stick to shake the branches and maybe separate them. The sound of their fighting fills the air. Screeches and squawks of aggression, squeals and screams of fear and pain. One has fallen. It lies bloody and broken on the ground at the far side of the shrub. I struggle toward it, to try to save it. But the aggressor still attacks, driving its hooked beak again and again into the flesh, ripping and tearing and piercing. "Shoo," I call at the flapping sun bird, "Shoo." I flail at him. He still continues with his pecking and his destruction. The victim is lying very still, but the attacker still pecks at him, not satisfied even with the death of his foe. I reach the little dead bird and lift his body in my hand. For an instant, I am almost afraid of the live one, afraid that I too will be attacked. But he flies away.

The dead sun bird lies in the palm of my hand, its metallic green feathers, its bright yellow and purple breast feathers broken and hacked and soaked in blood. It is little more than three inches long. This image carries too much baggage from the past. Tears well up, uncontrollably, and mingle, like the saint's did, with the blood of the bird. I fling the little body from me as far away as possible. And turn to find Irungu watching me, watching over me, as he seems to do these days.

"Ah, this one," he says. "It will protect its home and its female. Any other male who tries to come in will be killed. That is the way."

As I walk wearily up the steps to the patio, I hear the sound of raised voices from the sitting room beyond. I pull back the glass doors and Shiku and Julius stand there, startled, their argument stopped in mid-phrase. Julius gives me a look of disdain and barges out. I hear the bang of a car door, the rev of an engine, the beep of the horn for Irungu to open the gates. Shiku hasn't moved. She dabs at her eyes with the undersides of her hands. Tries to smooth down her hair which has sprung free from its plaits. Her face is swollen. I wonder if he has slapped her. I am, at the same time, angry at him, outraged for her and indignantly protective. Yet somewhere in me is a tiny spark of optimism, because, if they are falling apart, then maybe there is hope for me.

"Julius is going up country on a field trip. He wants you to go with him."

"Me? How can I?"

"He will not leave you here with me. If you refuse to go, he will be suspicious."

"This is ridiculous. How can he expect me—?"

Shiku has burst into tears. "Please, Ciarán, if I mean anything to you, for my sake. Go."

14

Irungu salutes as we pass through the big black gates. Peponi Road is ordinary. Like any suburban street. Cars, buses, and pickup trucks chug slowly along on the macadam road. Hordes of people walk along the dusty roadside tracks. Groups gather around the wayside shacks that sell groceries and cigarettes. A man is bringing pot plants down to water at the stream that feeds his nursery garden. As we are stalled in traffic at the bridge, a woman passes us carrying a crate of Coca-Cola balanced hands-free on her head. Julius sees her too, chuckles with satisfaction and catches my grin with a sidelong glance.

Today he is sporting a huge Texan hat that he brought back with him from the United States. He is wearing leather cowboy boots and his feet must be sweltering.

"Snakes," he says.

"What?"

"A thick pair of boots is a great protection against snakes where we're going."

Had I really looked so obviously at his feet? This man is scrutinizing me too closely. Why? For the first time, a little guilt surfaces in me and I am afraid that he will sense it. I look out the window, away from him. Why should I feel guilty? I battle with myself. He was the one who went away and abandoned them.

The traffic worsens. We stop and start in a queue of cars on a roundabout. Suddenly, a face is at the window. A pair of hands reaches in through the gap above the glass. I see a blade, a *panga*. I cry out, terrified.

"*Toka, toka!*" Julius shouts and leans across me to wind up the window. Startled, the face moves back from the glass; hands are withdrawn. I see that it is just a boy, a ragged street child. The glint of metal that I saw was a dustpan he had been trying to sell to me. Most likely, he had made it himself out of a recycled tin can. Nothing goes to waste here. I watch as he runs off to try his wares elsewhere. His smell lingers in the car—a unique blend of human excrement and glue. I am quivering with fright.

Julius looks at me, opens his mouth as if to say something, then closes his mouth again and shakes his head. "In the old days, these boys would have been sent out to the forest or the bush to become warriors. Nowadays, they are sent to the city, to starve and steal and sniff glue. It is a strange aberration."

I feel grateful to him for not drawing attention to my panic. It was embarrassing enough without comments, either cynical or calming.

A small, four-seater airplane is fueled and ready for us. Julius gives me a helping hand to clamber inside. Then he takes his own place beside the pilot. I'm glad that he hasn't squeezed into the seat beside me. His big bulk would seem doubly intimidating at this proximity. The back of his head and the tycoon's hat are a much more comforting sight. He and the pilot are jabbering away in some language that I do not know. It is not Swahili or Kikuyu. Luo, maybe. Yes, the pilot introduced himself with a Luo name. I am pleased to be so utterly excluded from the conversation. It is funny, but since this morning, since we left the house and compound, I feel different. More optimistic, if that's possible. Although I still can't begin to think about any moment other than this one, the now is suddenly interesting.

If the plane should crash . . . That same old thought surfaces as it always does. If the plane should crash I will go back there. I will be happy. The mantra hasn't changed that much. It is just that "there" was alone. Which makes here and now godless, unpredictable, without plan or providence. Yet, it goes on. Minute after minute, day after day, the now. And when it ends I will be happy. But am I not happy now?

The little plane thrusts itself forward with a great scream of its engine and throws itself up in the air. I look down, breathlessly and with thundering heart, at the scorched grass and reddish earth, so close below us, and sigh with relief as she holds and circles and climbs.

This is exciting. If I feel a sense of danger, maybe the old instinct for survival has not been lost after all. But, how different it is when you know where you are going.

As the city falls away below and behind us, we nudge northward over the neat, green beds of the tea plantations and the coffee farms. The great mountain is hiding, as usual, behind its cloak of clouds. We climb, higher and higher, to clear the edge of the Great Rift and suddenly, from here, a huge vista opens up, a landscape of unfathomable immensity. "Miles and miles of bloody Africa" was what the settlers called this vastness. And then they set out to discover, map, conquer, and claim each mile after bloody mile of it. I have been listening too much to Irungu. My guilt for the yoke of colonialism has become more personal. I am dreadfully afraid that what he says is true—that the process was aided by the "spiritual colonists"—men such as myself with the greatest of good intentions. When you take a man's religion, you take away his sense of place in the world. We, the Irish, of all people, should know that. Yet, from the earliest stirrings of Christianity in us, we carried our "true" faith everywhere we went as a gift to others, never asking what it was replacing.

The airstrip where we land is distinguishable only by the air sock that hangs, limp and empty, at one end. We bump and roll and slide to an ungainly stop on the rough surface. There is little sign of habitation around, just clusters of huts with straw roofs that taper up to a knotted twist on top. From the air, I saw a tangle of dust roads leading off to a wider, straighter road that must be a highway. Where are we? Feeling as I did, like a reluctant hostage on this excursion, I neglected to ask where we were going. Actually, I like the adventure of not knowing.

The pilot shakes us both by the hand and hastens off to return home while daylight lasts. I stand bemused, shaky on my feet, while Julius gathers the luggage and piles it into the back seat of an ancient Land Rover that is waiting for us. We both squeeze in beside the driver in the front. I am on the outside, and am jostled against the door as we rattle along the stony dirt track. Again, with amazing accuracy, my companion seems to read my mind. He pushes over on the seat to give me more room and puts a protective arm around me, holding me back from the door. His gentleness surprises me. I realize that I know very little about this man. Whatever images I have formed of him are uninformed by any real knowledge. I have always cut across any mention of him by Shiku.

We come to the main road which is bordered, at this point, by a straggle of wooden and concrete buildings, each with a broad awning at the front. It is stifling hot and I am coated all over and choking with dust. A sign above one of the doors reads: *pombe baridi—bia na bora.* "Cold beer—the best beer." Julius signals to the driver to pull in and tells him to bring the luggage on to our *hoteli*, which is up the street.

"A drink?" he asks.

"Yeah." A drink would be welcome. There is cold beer and hot, roast chicken. The mingling smells are mouth-watering. Julius orders both and I think, suddenly, about money and the fact that I have none to pay my share. Am I still on the Church payroll? I wonder. Is there money accumulating in a bank account, or have I been struck off? Hardly, without notification. I have heard nothing since my act of insubordination.

"Julius," I say timidly, "I'm sorry, but I have no money on me now." I feel like a sponger. "I'll pay you back when . . ."

"Yes," he says. "I suppose you didn't think of taking money with you when you were being carried off, unconscious, to hospital."

"I certainly didn't think I'd need it where I was going."

"Don't worry. You would do the same for me. And maybe, sometime, you will. Cheers!"

"*Sláinte.*"

By now my eyes have adjusted to the dim light, and I become aware that I am being watched. There is a woman sitting at a small table in the corner; her gaze never wavers from me. I feel embarrassed. Look away. Engage myself with other things, like the thick glass tumblers stacked up behind the bar, the water jugs for washing hands. The barman is also the chef and has disappeared outside to tend the roasting chicken. Inadvertently, I catch her eyes again. She says something that I don't understand, apart from the word Coca-Cola.

"Ah, the lady is thirsty," Julius declares and bangs the counter for service. The Coke is brought and the woman presses her breasts and stomach against me as she collects it.

"You have an admirer." Julius is hugely amused.

A conversation passes between him and the woman.

"Thank you," she says to me in English. "Thank you for the drink."

"You're welcome."

A brief conversation follows between them and she brushes against me again as she takes the drink back to her table. "You, me, later," she says, and smiles.

The roast chicken is marred by her watchful eyes on me all the time while I eat. What has Julius said to her? I envy him the ease with which he inhabits this polyglot world, shifting from language to language as readily as he would change a shirt.

When the chicken has been cleared away, the conversation begins again, this time in English, for my benefit. "This is my friend, Kilani. He is a European." Julius signals to the girl and she comes and hovers beside me. "He will pay good money for a woman like you." He takes a bank note out of his pocket and places it on the counter under my hand. "You like this man? We will make a bargain, yes? A fine woman, don't you think, Kilani? Great big bottom. Wonderful breasts. Child-bearing hips. Better than what I have at home. What d'you say?"

The girl giggles and rubs her hips up against me. Disgust shows on my face. I can judge that by her reaction.

But the teasing continues. "What is wrong, Kilani? You don't like African women?" To her, he says, "I think he only likes white women."

The dark eyes look offended.

"No." I scramble for some excuse. How can I explain to her about celibacy, about morality? "I'm . . ." the familiar excuse reaches my tongue: "I'm a priest."

"Ah, Kilani doesn't like white women, either. He doesn't know what to do." The mockery is just too blatant. He knows.

Julius picks the note from the counter and stands up, giving a conspiratorial wink and a nod toward the woman. I watch, helplessly, as they leave together, his hand possessively straddling her broad, wagging buttocks.

I am left with my indignation and the unpaid bill. "Boss," I call to the barman. "Another beer, please."

I decide to drink myself into oblivion, so that if Julius does not come to rescue me, I will at least be spared the shame. As the beer goes down, glass after frothy glass, I cheer up. I smile. Perhaps I will drink myself to death and find myself again where I was.

The evening customers come and go, eyeing me suspiciously. I converse heartily in English, talking to them, but mostly to myself. An odd grin or nod shows that not all I say is lost on them, but they do not talk to me. I buy them drinks. My voice rises above theirs and I launch, loudly, into a verse of a song. "Molly Malone" is the one that comes to me. In the chorus, other voices join mine. I stop and they carry on. They know the words. "Ah," I shout, delighted. "You can't beat an Irish education."

Irish. Irish. The word reverberates around the room. Something is understood. People come and slap me on the back. "Ah, Irish." I buy a drink for the bar.

Our revelry is interrupted by a figure standing in the open doorway. My heart sinks at the sight of the Texan hat. I am only halfway to oblivion.

"Good God!" he exclaims. "I forgot all about you. Are you okay?" He stops, aware of the silence that has fallen and the smiling faces and full glasses all around.

"You forgot to pay your bill," I tell him and hand him the chit.

He peruses the list of figures and nods his head toward the barman. "Are you being cheated here, Kilani?"

"No," I answer. "Nobody's been cheating here, except maybe yourself."

Julius looks from me to the barman to the other patrons and throws his head back in a loud laugh. Then he says to me in a broad Yankee drawl, "I declare, Kilani, but you got guts." He hands over the money, plus a tip.

Outside, the drunkenness hits me and I have to lean

against him for support. He bears the weight willingly, without fuss. "Thank God," he says. "If I lost you, my wife would never speak to me again."

"Your wife?" I slur, foolishly. "You care about your wife?"

His pace speeds up and his boots have a heavy, angry tread on the ground. He says nothing, but drags me now, rather than supporting me. We reach the *hoteli* and our room. He strips off his clothes and stands naked beside his bed.

"What's the matter with you? Have you a problem with this, *Father*?" He jigs and thrusts his genitals in an obscene way. "You have a problem with women?" His eyes look through me as if he sees everything.

I am disgusted by this strutting, peacock display. My mind conjures a picture of his unholy copulation with the woman from the bar. And the face in the vision, inevitably, changes to Shiku's. I see him fucking her. That is what he does. It is a violation. I have no doubt.

Without thinking, I have begun to undress. Julius stops mid-strut and gasps, staring open-mouthed at my scars. "Way-ay-ay! Irungu has done you much damage." He changes suddenly from peacock to mother hen, remembering his responsibilities to me. "I was told to keep you free of fevers. And malaria."

Already, I am swatting at a mosquito that is worrying my neck. Julius lunges into his bag and takes out a mosquito-repellent coil. "My wife always packs these, but I never use them myself." He puts a match to the spiral and blows out the flame so that there is just a glow remaining. The scented smoke wafts through the room. His nakedness forgotten, he tucks me up in bed as if I were an invalid. Then he pads softly over to the light switch and back to his own bed.

"It isn't sex—it's love that celibacy denies. Maybe you're the one who has a problem with women."

His answer is like a sigh in the darkness: "Maybe I am."

In the morning, the smell of cooking food nauseates me. There seems to be a little man with a hammer-drill working away inside my head. But Julius fusses over me and insists that I eat a good breakfast. "You'll need it for the journey ahead. We'll be rocking about in these Jeeps on rough roads for several hours."

"Jeeps?"

"We're going in convoy. It's safer that we travel together."

Food, spare tires, petrol, and other supplies are packed in beside the *pangas*, rakes, brushes, canvas, tent poles, and sleeping bags in the rugged old Land Rover. The back seats have been taken out and the whole space has been filled. I think of yesterday's uncomfortable journey and I quail. But Julius jumps up into the driver's seat, adjusts his mirrors and driving position and signals me to get in. I have the whole of the passenger's seat to myself. "You can sleep if you want," he says and reaches into the back for a pillow. This is luxury.

As we drive slowly up the road, other vehicles emerge from the side roads, as if there has been some invisible signal. All are basic Land Rovers, the same as our own. No doubt they have proven their worth in this rough terrain, but I guess that another reason for the uniformity is the interchangeability of spare parts. Soon there are six or eight of us driving together, one behind the other, and sending up a huge cloud of dust in our wake.

We pass by occasional villages, groups of huts clustered together, all with that same air of being at once ancient and transient. Most of the more permanent structures are schoolhouses and churches. Children in school uniforms flock along the edges of the road. Catching sight of my white face in the window, they raise their fingers, pointing excitedly: "*Mzungu, mzungu.*" White man.

We see occasional signs of animal life. Heaps of elephant dung are scattered on the road in one spot. A dik-dik bounds ahead of us into the scrub. Along a dried-up river bed, a giraffe munches on the succulent leaves of trees whose roots find water way below ground. Nests of weaver birds hang, like crazy Christmas decorations, on the branches of the flat-topped acacia trees. But, as we go on, the land becomes drier, supporting fewer species and less vegetation. Acacias become stunted and look more like bushes than trees. Termite mounds, like chimneys, rise higher than most of the growing things. The convoy stops. "What is it?" the shouted message goes to the front. Back comes the word: "*Nyoka.*" A massive boa constrictor is slithering its way across the road ahead and we are waiting to let it pass.

We pause in a quiet place, to make a toilet stop. As we relieve ourselves, heads bob up out of the bushes in front of us. Some little children have spotted our dust trail and crept up beside the road to watch us go by.

Further on, a group of *morans*, in their regalia and with their spears by their sides, stand tall and fierce-looking, guarding their territory. "If only . . ." Julius says out of the blue.

"If only what?" I am half afraid of what his answer may be, but he seems to be looking at the young warriors with vague longing on his face, so I risk the question.

"If only I could have been a *moran*. My mother's people were Maasai. Perhaps, if she had never met my father . . ."

"If your mother hadn't met your father, you wouldn't exist. And anyway, they're not Maasai, are they?"

Julius' belly is quivering with suppressed laughter. "You're too smart for me, Kilani. They're not Maasai. But the tradition of sending the young men out to fend for themselves is the same. They have to perform feats of bravery and survival. The weak ones don't come back."

"Wasn't it unusual for a Kikuyu to marry a Maasai woman?"

"They married soon after Independence, when there was a great feeling of hope and of openness between tribes. My father was an admirer of Julius Nyerere. And he was impressed by Nyerere's efforts to break down tribalism in his own country, by banning tribal dress and introducing integrated education."

"That's why he called you Julius."

"And that's why I was always reminded that I was of mixed tribe and a better man because of it. And why I would never have been allowed to wear tribal dress and be a *moran*."

"But you don't resent white people for changing the way of life here?"

"For trying to take what was not theirs, yes. But for changing it? No. Change is a necessary part of us. And education, the white man's magic, is something we have taken and perfected for ourselves. No, I would not give up the life I have so that I could carry a spear and defend my cows and women." The last part of his speech has brought him round to a place he had forgotten. We continue on in silence.

We are driving beside an expanse of silver-and-blue water, shimmering in the sun. Tall, stately trees grow beside it and cast their reflections on the surface.

"Look, Julius! Isn't that beautiful?"

"Have you a camera?"

"No. Why?" But, even as I ask, I realize that there is something strangely ethereal about the beauty of this lake. Enthralling and seductive as it is, this is only an illusion.

Suddenly, it is gone. There is nothing there but desert and a few stunted thorns. We don't even have a photograph to prove we've seen it. All that is left of that vision is the memory if it, etched on my inner eye.

"How can you photograph something that isn't real?"

"The atmospherics would deceive the lens as they did the eye."

For a while, I carry it with me, for awhile, as real, or unreal, as it was. I keep imagining it at each new turn of the road, across each desert landscape. The mirage seems an apt symbol for my life just now. My vision of Heaven, enticingly displayed, then grasped away. My Catholic vision of the world, melting before my eyes. My love for Shiku unsustainable, especially since Julius' return. My vision of my future, as uncertain and elusive as that glittering lake. Take a step toward it and it retreats, dries up, leaves you stranded in the blistering heat.

I wedge my pillow up against the door of the car, find myself a semi-comfortable position, lulled by the motion of the Jeep and too tired, even, to be bothered by the lurching and joggling. The convoy stops, now and again, to change a tire on one or other vehicle. Between us we have plenty of spares. Luckily, Julius and I are saved the inconvenience of a puncture. I sleep.

"Kilani, Kilani!" I am shaken awake. "Kilani, look!"

As I open my eyes, I see another mirage. Greeny-blue

this time and with the dark peaks of an island hanging between it and the sky. It is breathtaking, with that eerie quality of the first one. Even as I look, it changes through a succession of colors, from opaque blue to emerald, to jade green. The mountains behind seem to shift and change color, too.

"I won't be fooled this time."

My companion is bent over the steering wheel, laughing. "Kilani, it's real. Your first view of the lake. I had to wake you up to see it."

I can see that he is bubbling with excitement, that he had to wake me because he needed to share this moment with someone. Again, I am thrown back to the strange enigma of this man whom I hardly know. Stretching and yawning, I blink myself properly awake and look out across the unexpectedly real waters stretching on for miles and miles. A thrill of something vaguely like joy washes through me.

"Anyway," I ask. "What is it we've come here to find?"

"Our ancestors."

"Yours or mine?"

"The same."

"Really? And were they black or white?"

"Black, of course." He gives me a huge, satisfied smirk, watching my reaction as he says: "It was you guys who went off to whiten your skins and grow hairy in the far north, away from the center of the universe where we all began."

Knowing Julius' penchant for exaggeration, I hold my judgement on this one, but I am fascinated just the same. Nobody has ever suggested to me that such a version of events might even be considered.

We reach our destination just before dark and we all take a hand in pitching the tents. It is a difficult task, as we are buffeted by a strong wind and the light is gone before we finish. I am exhausted after my journey and last night's excesses, so I make my excuses and go to the tent that I will share with Julius. The dinner that is being served up doesn't look too savory, anyway. And I don't feel up to joining in the camaraderie and chitchat that is going on in the mess tent. As I zip myself into a sleeping bag, Julius comes in and lights a mosquito coil and places a bunch of plants at the door flap. He explains that these will repel snakes, so I will be perfectly safe and I may sleep without worry. "And the crocodiles around here are not man-eaters, so there is no need to worry about them, either."

It's still dark when I wake. Julius is already up and dressed and breakfasted. "Stay in bed if you want to," he says, "but I won't waste an hour or a minute of daylight." I hop out of bed and follow him outside just in time to see the sunrise over the Rift. The sun comes up quickly in a great pink ball. It sheds its rays across the valley and the lake and mountains, striking color into everything. This is the first of many sunrises. I bear witness to every one of them. It becomes my morning ritual, a little homage that I pay to the coming day.

A week or more passes. Each day I walk by the lakeshore and monitor the moods and shifts of those waters. They are ever-changing. Once, as I stand there, the lake turns dark and choppy and a big wind and squall of rain blows up with such suddenness and ferocity that it startles the basking crocodiles, and drenches me to the skin.

Among the birds there, I see a flock of swallows on their migration north. Perhaps they will wing their way to Ireland from here. Establishing dual citizenship. Half black, half white. Did some of these hatch from the nest in the eaves of my mother's house? I wonder. I remember, as a teenager, envying them their wings to fly south to this place where I wanted to be but could not yet go. There is something of the wonder of that boy awakening in me. Questions hammer, one against the next, and I revel in the beauty of the questions themselves, enjoying the mystery of what they might contain, without really worrying about answers.

I lose track of days. It is a time of rest. Rejuvenation is the word that presents itself and finds its way on to my page.

"What is it you're always writing?" Julius asks.

"I don't know. It started as a memoir. Then it became fiction. I thought that I had finished, but I suspect I never will."

At sundown, everyone congregates in the mess tent for dinner and beers. But, despite the wind, I prefer to sit outside where I can watch the stars and smell the hot smell of the earth and hear the stirrings of birds and goats, people and animals. From here I see Orion, not upright as he is in the northern hemisphere, but lying on his side, his quiver neither up nor down. It is nice to think that even constellations of stars can look different, depending on your vantage point.

This evening Julius brings out a small table and an extra chair from the mess tent and brings out a beer for me as well as for himself. "You're right, Kilani. It's nice out here."

"Did you dig up anything interesting today?"

"A fossilized fragment of a skull. It could be hominid. We'll have to wait and see, but it's a start."

Ah, so this is the reason for this evening's friendliness. He is in celebratory mood. Yet, here he is sitting with me instead of sharing the excitement of the find with his colleagues inside.

He blinds me for a while with archaeological jargon. I follow most of it, but it is too much hard work here, in this place and at this time. And I haven't drunk any beer since the night in the bar, so it is making me feel heady.

Julius' conversation drifts and spins into the stories that he loves to tell. This time, he is going on about the Irish. Apparently, one time, an Irish farmer who lived in this country had the effrontery to name his bull after the late President. His Excellency heard of it, and the farmer was deported.

I laugh.

"See," he says, as if I have proven the point of his story. "You are all the same. You have no sense of decorum. No respect."

"But," I protest, "any Irishman could tell you that naming the bull was not an act of disrespect. It was the opposite. What he was saying was that he admired the President for his power." I pause. "And for his balls and neck. Which, to an Irishman, means courage and strength."

Julius nearly chokes over his beer. "Balls and neck," he repeats, laughing.

"Now, if it were an Englishman who had called his bull after the President, then he would deserve deportation."

Julius' laughter booms loud in the silence. "You know, Irish, I can't stop myself from liking you, much as I don't want to let myself."

"That's mutual."

15

My curiosity takes me out to the excavation site. Julius is delighted that I have made the effort. It gives him an opportunity to enthuse about his work and to show me what they are doing. The team is tediously brushing away the silt and the black, volcanic pebbles in which their archaeological treasure may be stored. They pause, momentarily, to greet me. Then they turn their full attention back to what they are doing. Their dedication and enthusiasm are impressive. Julius explains that digging is impossible at this stage because some of the skull fragments may be quite tiny or might be damaged by a careless thrust of a sharp tool.

"At the time this guy died, the lake would have extended as far as here. The reason the skull, or part of it, was preserved, was because it lay in a shallow lagoon and was covered with silt, and fossilized."

"Has the lake dried up that much?"

"The level is never constant—a fact that seemed to have escaped the notice of some Europeans who organized a fishery here some years back." He laughs. Racially superior. "If they had asked us, we might have told them that this lake has shrunk and grown, shrunk and grown. It even dried up completely at some stage in its history. The docks and boats are still there, several hundred meters from the water."

As we talk, we walk to the lakeshore. Julius points out fossils and evidence of different water levels over the years and the millennia. He reaches down and takes my hand in his. It is clammy with sweat. This is a gesture I have seen many times among tribesmen. A sign of friendship. Our hands, together, are warm and wet. I feel myself shrinking beside him. Growing small. I look up at the tall man striding beside me and I feel safe, safer than I have been for a long time. I think of my hand in my father's hand all those years ago. It is the same feeling. He will be my father now. I will be his son and he will keep me safe. He will ward off the emptiness that threatens to swamp me. And this time, this time, I will be a good son.

"There is a wonderful story about Enkai, the god of the Maasai. Once there was a terrible drought. There was no food for the cattle and they were dying in huge numbers. The Maasai people were starving. And so a group of warriors was sent to speak to Enkai. They had to travel great distances in a ravished land until they came to the holy mountain of the Maasai. That place is very far south of here. And the mountain is a volcano that spits fire and smoke and makes loud noises. Not as tranquil a place as the sacred mountain of the Kikuyu. Enkai spoke in a low, rumbling voice. 'The reason why your people are dying is because you have been too busy warring with your neighbors and so have stayed too long in the one place. Your cattle are overgrazing your pastures. It is time to make peace with your neighbors and move on.'"

I smile at the story. "Your god of the Maasai is a god of the environment. Giving sound practical advice to his people."

"Most of the African peoples understand—or understood—the fragile balances that keep us here. Even the Sahara desert, one time, was a region of lakes and rivers where people lived and fished. As the land dried out, they moved out, some to more fertile places where they took up farming, others to lakes as far away as Lake Victoria and the Rift, where they could continue fishing. Some stayed, to keep cattle beside the few watering holes. Others, like the Tuaregs, became raiders and traders, exploiting the barrenness and isolation of the place and the vulnerability of their neighbors. Adaptation and change are the very nature of this place and its people."

Julius has stopped talking. That is unusual. There is just the sound of the crickets and the tree frogs. Shrill, soothing sounds. I am lulled by them. Lulled and comforted by the large and clammy hand that clasps mine. I forget that we are rivals. And, soon, I know that it is no longer he who holds my hand but I who hold his. Willingly, trustingly. I hope that he won't let mine go, won't abandon me to the emptiness of self.

Is this what I long for, then? To belong somewhere, anywhere, with someone? As son? As friend to this man? Was it the same belonging that I needed with Shiku? Not ownership, as she claimed, but belonging?

The big man stops in his striding. Hands still holding, he half turns toward me. His eyes are troubled. I had not expected that. And his words, when he speaks them, almost stop my heart still.

"My wife is pregnant."

Stupefied, I ask: "How? Who?"

Julius withdraws his hand and looks at me as if I am some kind of imbecile. "Well, I presume there wasn't anybody else in my absence."

"There was nobody else."

"Do you intend to steal her from me?"

"No." I am finding my way around these immense feelings that have burst in on me. There is ecstatic joy, coupled with a stark sense of loss. "No. Shiku would never be happy with me. I've nothing to offer her—them. It is you who Shiku wants."

He lets the air out of his mouth in a lingering sigh. We turn back toward the site. He takes up my hand again. Becomes father again—this time lecturing a wayward son. "Under the traditional laws, it might have been my privilege to share my wife, or wives, with you.

But, with my permission and on the understanding that you would not attempt to take her away from me, but these customs were replaced by your laws of God. Not only have you flouted our traditions, you have desecrated a union that you yourself made sacred."

Guilt, like a homing pigeon, finds its roost. His version of what happened is undeniably the truth, although until now, I could never have seen it that way.

"I have no defense, Julius. All I can do is give you my word that it is finished." But nothing, neither guilt nor the loss of Shiku, can stifle the surge of hope that is now buoying me up. There will be some part of myself left in the world when I go. I look up with admiration at the man beside me. Although he is twelve years my junior, he seems infinitely wiser than I. He is smiling quietly to himself. I realize that I too am smiling.

A shout from the excavation site reaches us and Julius runs ahead in response. By the time I reach there, the men are gathered in an excited bunch around him. On seeing me, one man triumphantly holds up what looks like a thick chunk of brown bone. They gather me into the group.

"Is it significant?"

"Might be. Might not be," Julius answers. The cautionary "might not be" is not reflected by the expressions on the faces of his colleagues. They are overjoyed at this find.

Still, the painstaking sifting and sorting continues.

They find nothing over the next days. I come across Julius puzzling over the precious fragments, assembling and disassembling them, searching for some pattern. Only he knows what, exactly, he is looking for. He scratches his head in frustration and starts again.

"If you found what you're looking for, would it make sense of the whole thing?"

"Maybe. What I'm at here, although it's scientific, is actually quite instinctive. The end results may or may not fit the pattern I think I'm looking for."

"Is this skull human?"

"Not human, exactly. Human-like, definitely, as opposed to ape-like. But whether it was an ancestral or a related strain, I just don't know."

"Yet."

"I might never gather enough evidence to find out for sure."

Julius is dipping a brush into a pot of glue and plastering it over the bits of bone. "I am sure–almost sure–that this is how it should go." He sticks one of the larger pieces to another, then fits in some of the tiny fragments. I watch in amazement as the object takes shape under his skilled fingers.

The tent flap opens and one of the team appears with another piece of jaw bone. "I think you are needing this one?" He grins. And when the bone is washed and glued, the emerging face grins, too.

Julius explains that we are missing the frontal eyebrow

sections, which would be vital for a proper identification. Neither do we have any of the tell-tale sections from the back of the skull that would indicate whether this creature walked upright. He is taking pains to translate all this into simple terms that I can understand, unlike our early discussions, when he tried to blind me with jargon. I am no longer being excluded.

What is left on the table is a collection of tiny fragments that seem impossible to place.

The glue has dried now and Julius places the skull in my hands. "Here, Kilani, what do you think?"

"How old is this?"

"We'll have to verify it, but I'd say something in the region of one point seven to two million years old."

I feel the smooth, hard texture of the fossilized bone, mahogany brown. I run my fingers along teeth that once chewed and smiled, round the bottom circles of the sockets out of which eyes once looked. "I believe it is my ancestor. A pre-human. One that was neither black nor white."

"Why are you so sure?"

"I feel it in my bones. Somewhere deep inside, it makes me feel ancient—as if I am connecting to some source."

"You're talking as a priest rather than a scientist. But I believe you are right. Even though, as an anthropologist, I cannot know."

"I can no longer talk as a priest."

"What is it then, that connects you with this?"

"A . . ." These words are slow. Difficult to formulate. "Some sense of belonging to something greater than myself. Like the skull, maybe. As if the whole is greater than the sum of the parts. I'm not very articulate, I'm afraid."

"What connects us to our ancestors is spirit."

"I don't believe in spirit."

"Father Ciarán, every word you speak, every breath you breathe, everything about you is spiritual."

With great care, I put the skull back on the table. "That part of my life is over."

In the evening, we sit outside under the stars. He tells me about the first white man ever seen in these parts—a missionary on his way to Uganda. The people could not understand that it was only his color that was different to theirs. They thought that it was the absence of skin that made him white. They called him "the man with no skin."

"The story, as I always heard and understood it, was that the man was killed because the people were afraid. But lately, I heard another version of it. It seems that his superior, a Scottish engineer-turned-missionary, asked the king of the Buganda for safe passage for his colleague, to get him through the 'badlands.'

"But the king was playing the Protestant missionaries against the Catholic, committing himself to neither, vacillating between them both, favoring one creed one week and persecuting it the next. That particular week must have been a good one for Catholics, because the deputation that was supposed to save the 'man with no skin' was sent with orders to kill him. I am sure that the poor man died thinking we were a most inhospitable people. Really, he was just a pawn in some unfathomable political game."

"I'm sure that didn't bother him," I answered. "He was too busy coming to terms with being dead."

A pucker of a smile is tugging up the corners of Julius's lips. "How would you know, Kilani?"

"Because I died."

He looks at me, halfway between incredulity and amusement. "Where did you go?"

"Heaven, maybe."

"But maybe yours is not the same place where a Protestant minister would go?"

"Ah, don't mock me. There's no real difference."

"Your people seem to make a big enough difference about it."

"That's not religion. It's tribalism."

"And was Heaven up there, where the white man says it is?"

"I don't think so. It didn't feel like that."

"Then maybe it was down, in the earth, where the spirits of the ancestors dwell."

"It might have been. But it wasn't spiritual at all."

"But if you were really dead, with what did you experience it?"

He has baited me. Backed me into a corner. Julius is a powerful debater. Perhaps he is trying to push me back into my old and, according to his concerns, safe role, but I suspect that these arguments are motivated by genuine interest or even empathy.

"You are a priest, Ciarán. I have met others like you. In other religions, even. It is not something that you put on and off when you remove a collar. It is something that you are."

His spiritual challenge is unexpected. I do not appreciate it from him. As I go back to the tent, I find anger in myself against him.

I am a fisher of the Sahara, come too late. I am the man with no skin—a harbinger, come too early. But I am not a priest.

The area all around the place where the skull fossils were found has now been excavated. Nothing more surfaces. The missing parts of the skull may have been exposed some time in the past: dug up by animals, brought to the surface by water, eroded or washed away. Julius is anxious to get back to the city. There is paperwork to be done. Conclusions to be drawn from this inconclusive find.

A small aircraft flies in to pick us up. The other team members are left to pack tents and equipment and to drive the convoy back. We take our leave of them and of the ever-changing lake.

***

The mirror shows a different face. Sun-tanned. Deeply lined, as if all the places that I have been to and seen are etched there. But there is something more permanent in the set of it. Perhaps my conviction that the future is something that will happen without me is not, exactly, a certainty. But I still can't see a place for myself in it.

Although my hostess is charming, I can't escape the feeling that I am intruding here. Every time she moves and the cloth of her dress straightens across her expanding stomach, I can feel my eyes alighting there, curious and anxious about my child. But I am peripheral to the household. They would rather be alone.

I seek out the company of Irungu in the garden. He greets me with the handshake of his tribe. Hands together, thumbs up together, clasp and hold. There is nothing half-hearted in his pleasure at seeing me.

"I am going to Kishagi, to my wife, Wambui. She will take me home to live." He does not say "to die." He has grown shockingly thin.

"That's good, Irungu. Wambui is a very forgiving woman."

"Such forgiveness does not come easily. Not without a price."

"What price is that?"

"I am to build her a stone house."

"What about your woman here?"

"She will be all right. That woman can make more

money in one night than I can earn in a month." He grins mischievously at me.

I caution him to "Tell her she must use condoms."

"Ah, she knows this. But the men do not want that. Especially the Europeans. Some will even pay more to do it without them." He chuckles loudly. "They will catch their own disease. They will cull themselves."

Whatever private reconciliation may have happened between myself and Irungu, my race will not be forgiven. And if, on some future occasion, the odds should stack themselves against me as they did before, I suspect that Irungu could and would do again what he has done. There are thousands of others like him who would do the same. I think of my own country's troubled relationship with the British.

"Is it an awful burden, Irungu, to know that you have AIDS?"

"How can a man worry about something that can take months or years to happen? Today, I could die of starvation, I could be killed in a crash on these roads, I could be murdered, I could get malaria. He is a lucky man who can know for sure that he will get through this day. And I have children. I have healthy sons. My spirit will have some place to rest.

"We are going to rebuild the market," he tells me. "Mzee Njuguna was asking me where you were and if you will come and help us."

"Where is Kariuki?"

"He is gone. Always, he was afraid for his life after what happened. They say he has gone to become a real priest, like you."

I *am* a real priest. In my heart and soul, I know that I can be nothing else. Officially, I have not been disciplined or struck off, as far as I know. An image comes into my head of Father Madden trying to tell the bishop what I have said. How can Madden explain it? Or the bishop understand?

Perhaps I will never again say Mass or administer a sacrament. To do so might be wrong or immoral. But was my ministry, before this, made worthy only because it was blinkered? A single view in a world of broader horizons?

Irungu runs to answer the gate and a white pickup truck pulls in. It is Nicolas. His face is as welcome a sight as I have seen in a long time. His broad smile of greeting is accompanied by a backslapping thump that knocks the breath out of me. "Baba Kilani, when are you coming home?"

"Whenever you're ready, Nicolas." The answer surprises me as much as it delights him.

"We have been waiting."

Maybe the bishop will be pleased enough to have any priest to run such a "dangerous" parish. And I will weave stories for my people, myths that will connect them to their world and to their source—Ngai, Enkai,

Yahweh, God—the one to whom we give many names, but for whom no name is enough.

There is work to be done in rebuilding the Kishagi Market: funds to be raised, materials to be procured. And, in the process, I will ensure that Irungu fulfills his promise to Wambui.

Shiku tries to persuade Nicolas to stay overnight, but he will not be swayed. He will have a cup of tea, that's all. The work of today must be done while the day lasts, before darkness falls. There is no time for stalling, for thinking anymore. For changing my mind.

My things have not been unpacked. Precious possessions: memoirs, stories, and scraps of ideas. I am a writer. Perhaps that is a form of priesthood, too.

Nicolas takes my few belongings and throws them in the back. Irungu is already sitting in the front of the pickup, grateful for the lift.

The family gathers itself on the doorstep, surprised by this sudden departure. A little disappointed that Shiku's father is rushing away, instead of staying for his usual visit. Shiku presents her cheeks to be kissed and the first one to be kissed again. As we squeeze each other's hands, there are tears in her eyes. I turn and hug Muthoni and scratch Sungura under the chin.

"We will miss you, bwana Ciarán."

Julius, from behind, puts his arms around his wife and, with a protective gesture, holds her stomach in his hands. "I will see that this child of mine is never allowed beside a busy highway."

He comes forward. Takes my hand in the Kikuyu handshake. "*Rafiki.*"

"*Rafiki,*" I call him. Friend.